N. K.
Hd

HE HAD NO RIGHT TO DICTATE TO HER!

The door opened and Lars stood there, his face a mixture of relief and anger. "Thank God," he said. "Come in. You've had me worried."

"I can't imagine why," she said. "I merely went out for the evening. Don't look at me like that, Lars."

"I didn't realize my concern would be so irritating to you," he said dryly. "I just wanted to make sure you were all right...Where were you anyway?"

"At Skansen Island, having dinner with Gunnar Lindstrom."

"I thought you might wait until I returned and we could have gone out," he replied angrily.

"You weren't sure when you'd return. You told me so. You said it might be late." She paused and they glared at each other like two combatants.

"I'm not objecting to your going out, but to go out with Gunnar Lindstrom..." He shook his head hopelessly. "You're lucky you got home in one piece."

"Don't be ridiculous. He behaved like a gentleman and I'll probably go out with him again. I like him, Lars. We had a great time together."

"Oh, yes, I'm sure. I've heard when he wants to, he can charm the daylights out of anyone. Especially impressionable young newcomers to Stockholm!"

SUMMER IN STOCKHOLM

by Vanessa Cartwright

A MacFadden Romance/New York

A Macfadden Romance

Kim Publishing Corp.
440 Park Avenue South
New York, N.Y. 10016

Published by arrangement with the author.
Printed in the United States of America.

ISBN: 0-89772-058-X

CHAPTER 1

Spring had come early to Illinois, with the leaves budding joyfully on the trees and the flowers beginning to push their eager heads through the soil. The snow and ice had long since melted and the overcast skies had given way to a cloudless expanse of bright blue. This was unusual, Karen knew, but she felt it was a good sign: not only for everyone, but for herself in particular. A sign that blue skies were ahead for her, and she felt more than encouraged. After all, it had been a bad winter, both the weather and the events which had changed her life so dramatically.

Who would have thought she would be on her way to Europe, to start a new life, to put the past behind her? She certainly never dreamed she would have to endure such a traumatic disruption of her daily routine, her well-planned and orderly existence. And above all, she could never have anticipated the news that changed her from a carefree girl into a woman: the news that, when it came, she could hardly believe. Like millions of others, she read every year of people being trapped in an avalanche, of being swept down the precipitous Swiss slopes to their death; but like most people, Karen never felt such a tragedy could happen to anyone near and dear, especially her own father and mother. It was only the following day, when she picked up the Minneapolis Tribune and saw the brief, callous item, that she realized the phone call from the Swiss police had not been a horrible dream; and later, when the afternoon Star expanded the story, she knew there was no doubt. There were the pictures, not only of her parents, but of the massive slide which had come rumbling down the side of the mountain, sweeping everything before it in a white cloud of death and destruction, burying everything in its path for eternity.

"Mr. and Mrs. Rolf Christensen, prominent Minneapolis residents, were killed in an avalanche yesterday near Gstaad, Switzerland, where they had been vacationing for the winter. They are survived by their daughter, Karen; Mr. Christensen's brother, Niels, a lecturer in humanities at the University at Uppsala, Sweden; and Mrs. Christensen's sister, Miss Ingrid Dinesen, a resident of Chicago. A memorial service will be held at St. Patrick's Cathedral on Friday. All branches of the Christensen Farm Equipment Company will be closed today and tomorrow."

Yes, Karen had thought: close the business down as a gesture of respect and sorrow, but afterwards, it would be business as usual. After all, the business practically ran itself; which was how her father had been able to take off for three months in Europe each year, skiing and visiting Uncle Niels in Sweden.

And now the business would continue, she knew instinctively, despite her total ignorance of its operation. She had grown up knowing that she was blessed with a family whose income afforded them the very best that money could buy; but how the bank account was refueled each month, Karen had no earthly idea. The chain of stores stretched from Minneapolis all the way west to Seattle, making the name Christensen equally as well known to farmers as Allis-Chalmers or John Deere or any of the major suppliers of farm equipment and products that kept the wheels of agriculture turning.

But, after the shock and the sorrow had diminished into a hard knot in her memory, Karen realized that she had no desire to maintain a position as head of the company. She did not see herself assuming the role of a domineering female executive like Rosalind Russell in those old movies on the late show in TV. The idea was ridiculous. A girl with only two years of college and a burning desire to get her degree and explore the mysteries of anthropology would be totally lost among the computer-controlled labyrinth of the company her father had built up. Karen shared her concerns with Aunt Ingrid when she came to Minneapolis for the memorial services. Aunt Ingrid, as always, had taken charge of the situation without batting an eyelid.

"You're upset, child," she had said to Karen. "You come and stay with me in Chicago for a spell. Then make up your mind. Decisions are seldom wise when made under great pressure. Give yourself time to adjust. Then you'll be able to determine what you want to do."

"I just want to finish college," Karen had said.

"And rightly so. And after that, you have all the money in the world to do whatever you want to. Go to Greece and dig among the ruins. Go to Bora Bora and study the natives. Anything..." Aunt Ingrid's pale, pinched face had smiled knowingly, reassuringly—just like Karen's mother used to. They were so alike, they could have been twins, Karen thought, instead of being twelve years apart.

So Karen had gone to Chicago and stayed with her aunt in her small, comfortable cottage in Evanston. The peaceful surroundings and the wonderful, old-world garden had helped heal the wound in her heart, the incredible sense of loss she experienced for weeks afterwards. Then one day, almost as though a page in her life had turned again, she made the decision. "I want to sell the house in Minneapolis," she told Aunt Ingrid. "There are too many memories there. And I want to sell the company, too."

"You can't do that, child."

"Why not? It's mine, now, isn't it?"

"Yes, but..." Aunt Ingrid frowned helplessly, and tried to reason with Karen. But the girl's mind was made up. No, not the girl's—the young woman's, for in the months after the tragedy, Karen realized that she was no longer the spry teenager, able to indulge herself in whatever she wanted. She was now the sole remaining Christensen. Alone in the world, except for Aunt Ingrid and Uncle Niels. And almost overnight, she found herself thinking with a new maturity, a new ability to make decisions. And she knew her decision to sell was the right one.

And almost in answer to her prayers, there came the letter from Uncle Niels, offering her a home and an opportunity to complete her degree at the University at Uppsala. Aunt Ingrid had been upset at first, believing that Karen would stay with her; but eventually, Karen convinced her the move would be a wise one.

"I've never been to Sweden," she said. "I've always wanted to see where daddy's family came from. To visit the land. To get back to my roots, as it were. You understand?"

The older woman had nodded, aware that her niece was as stubborn as her father had been, once her mind was made up; she had the Christensen quality of forthrightness, of single-minded dedication to a project. Reluctantly, Aunt Ingrid helped with the endless details involved in disposing of the house in Minneapolis, the sale of the company, the thousand and one things to be handled before Karen could pack her suitcases and leave.

Amazingly, it had all been done in a matter of months. Winter had loosened its grip on the Midwest and spring was four weeks old by the time Karen finally called TWA and made her reservation to London. And now, at long last, the moment had come.

She went over the details in her mind for the hundredth time, excited, tremulous, anxious to be on her way. She would leave Chicago on Flight 506, departing at 7:30 in the evening, and arriving at Heath Row Airport at 9:00 the following morning. A brief layover, then at 12:55 she would leave on Scandinavian Air Lines on Flight 506, arriving at Arlanda Airport, 27 miles outside Stockholm, at 2:55. Uncle Niels would be able to meet her, as he only taught in the mornings. He had written and told her his last class let out at eleven, allowing him plenty of time to drive the 60 kilometers from Uppsala to Stockholm. And he had stressed again how much he was looking forward to seeing her again, and having her share his home. "You will be the daughter I never had," he wrote, a statement that touched Karen so much, she felt like breaking down and weeping with joy; for while she knew nobody would ever be able to replace her father, at least Uncle Niels would be the closest substitute she could ever find. Certainly far more agreeable than Aunt Ingrid who, despite her kindness and excessive efforts to please, was still an old maid, used to living alone. In time, Karen felt, her aunt would resent sharing her home with someone so much younger, so basically different in her outlook. It was the old story: differing generations seldom, if ever, manage to live together for very long without the inevitable clashes and confrontations. Karen was in no mood to have to put up with her aunt's peculiar idiosyncrasies.At least Uncle Niels was a little younger, more her father's age, and, from what she knew of him, a brilliant, progressively-minded, liberal man. She felt she would enjoy staying with him, even though she planned to get a place of her own eventually. She certainly had the money to do whatever she wanted. The winding up of the family estate, and the sale of the business, had left her enviably rich. Her lawyer had told her she would never have to worry about money again; which was a stupendous revelation. What young woman of twenty was blessed with such a situation? she thought, but then, how many lose both parents so early in life? Much as Karen was grateful for her inheritance, she would glady have given up every penny to have her mother and father back again.

She had finished her packing, making sure every last item was tucked away. She had gone to Marshall Fields and really splurged—not only the elegant looking set of matching leather luggage, but more than enough to fill the five suitcases. Aunt Ingrid had accompanied her, gasping with delight at the array of dresses that Karen selected, and always putting in a gentle suggestion that stemmed from her practical nature.

"Not the satin, dear...very difficult to keep clean," she said. "And the chiffon...well, I think that's a bit on the frothy side, wouldn't you say?" And on and on, until Karen found herself somewhat confused and unsure which garments to take. Finally, depositing Aunt Ingrid in the restaurant and making the excuse she was going to the restroom, Karen fled back to the dress department and, on her own, made up her mind in ten minutes, much to the salesgirl's amusement. She did, however, bear in mind that she would undoubtedly not be involved in too much social activity. She chose, therefore, two travel dresses of arnel jersey, and eight others that would be, she felt, suitable for almost any occasion: college, cocktails or an evening out with Uncle Niels. And, she reminded herself, there would undoubtedly come a time when some handsome young Swede would be calling on her, and her heart beat a little faster at the thought.

Karen had never really had a steady boy-friend, not since Kevin in high school, and that was more a teenage crush than anything serious. Kevin had been the football hero of the graduating class—

tall, dark, almost too handsome—and he had dated Karen several times. But after he discovered she was not as cooperative as some girls he knew, his interest in her cooled almost overnight. Karen had been mortified, but managed to get over her infatuation. She had decided very early in her teens that she was not going to go "all the way" as so many other girls did, winding up with the inevitable heartbreak, or, as happened in some cases, with a forced marriage, a baby and a divorce a year later. Her inherently practical nature, reinforced by occasional heart-to-heart talks with her mother made her realize that there would be plenty of time for serious romance after she had completed her schooling. And to Karen, the most important goal in her life was to get her degree and pursue the subject that had interested her ever since she could remember.

"Anthropology?" Even her father had questioned her choice of majors in college, wondering what it could be in such a dull subject to arouse the passionate interest of his daughter.

"It's not dull, daddy," she had explained more than once. "It's fascinating. Don't you ever wonder where we came from? Why the human race has evolved the way it has? There are some tribes in New Guinea who still live like stone age people. I want to go there one day and study them."

And her father had shaken his head hopelessly, given her a tolerant smile and let it go. As the years passed, he grew to understand Karen's deep devotion to history and the evolution of mankind, but he was far too busy with his own interests to question her in any great detail. "As long as you're happy, that's all that matters," was his favorite statement whenever they got into discussions about their respective pursuits.

It was only to be expected, therefore, that Karen found few boys at school who shared her academic interests; and when her passing infatuation with Kevin was over, she decided there would be no sense in wasting her time with boys who were only interested in how far they might be able to go with her.

That had been in school; but now...Karen realized that she had, in the six months since her parents' death, grown up considerably. There was no daddy to go to; no mama to have those intimate little chats with; she had only herself to rely upon. And her newfound feeling of womanhood seemed to spur an awareness of her undeniable attractions for the opposite sex.

As she dressed in readiness for her trip, she sat in front of the mirror in Aunt Ingrid's house, brushing her long, blond hair and admiring her reflection. Her eyes, deep blue like her father's had been, still held some sadness within their depths—an impression that could be quickly dispelled whenever she smiled, lifting the corners of her perfect mouth, bright red to the point that she never needed lipstick. She had, Karen decided, what could be called a perky face with an impish look to it that might even be called flirtatious. And why not? She was a young woman now—very self-possessed, independent and embarking on a new life in a new land. She lifted her chin, gave herself a penetrating glance of appraisal, and nodded.

"You're fine," she murmured to herself. "You're going to take Sweden by storm." Then she giggled, wondering what Aunt Ingrid would say if she heard her. Poor Aunt Ingrid! The woman had been painfully plain all her life. Combined with an unhappy love affair in her youth, her lifelong interest in religion had molded her into a rather autocratic and severe woman, not without kindness and compassion but nevertheless somewhat narrow in her attitudes towards the wayward ways of the world, which she regarded with an abiding suspicion. She had been personal secretary to the president of a large electronics firm in Chicago for over twenty years—dedicated to her work, and unrelenting in her adherence to the principle that all work and no play was the only enduring road to personal success in life. Karen sighed gratefully that she had escaped having to live with her aunt. The woman had been a great help, and a wonderful comfort in the weeks immediately after the tragedy—but Karen knew if they were to live together, there would be nothing but problems...

And she intended to have as few problems as she could in the future. She anticipated a carefree and productive period ahead, completing her degree, learning as much as she could about Sweden and its people. And if she found someone attractive, appealing...well, she wouldn't bar herself from becoming involved. Heaven knows, she did not envision herself winding up like Aunt Ingrid! Heaven forbid! Maybe there could even be an anthropology student at the University at Uppsala who would share her passionate interest as well as a little passion, perhaps...

Karen stood up, took a last look around the bedroom, nodded to herself, and walked into the livingroom. Aunt Ingrid was seated by the window, staring out at the flower beds with a contented expression on her thin, lined face.

"It makes me feel so wonderful," said her aunt. "This time of year. Everything is pushing up, reaching for life. In another few weeks, this will all be a mass of beauty. I wish you could be here to see it, Karen."

"I'll see the flowers in Stockholm," Karen replied brightly. "I'll send you some pictures."

"I'm going to miss you." The eyes that settled on Karen were pitiful in their plaintive sorrow.

"Now, now, Aunt Ingrid, no tears, please." Karen went across and embraced her aunt. "Try to be as happy as I am now. I'm actually beginning to feel rather excited."

"You're going to be so far away."

"It's only a few hours by plane. You can come and see me sometimes."

"Oh, I couldn't! I'd never ride in one of those jets. I'd be terrified out of my wits. It's bad enough having to go by car on the expressway." Aunt Ingrid managed a wan smile. "You must think me a terrible fuddy-duddy, but then, that's the way I am, child." She gave Karen's figure a quick glance of appraisal. "My, you do look nice."

"Thanks."

"Now you be careful. You will be staying at the airport in London between your flights, won't you?"

"Of course. I don't have time to gallivant around. There's only less than three hours between planes. I'll be all right, Aunt Ingrid. Please take that worried look off your face."

"I can't help it. When I think of you, leaving us for good, going halfway around the world..." Her voice broke and she sniffled loudly. Then she lifted her chin, making a determined effort to remain calm. "Anyway, give Uncle Niels my love.

Maybe I will come and visit you one day. By ship
of course. Much more civilized, I think."

Karen laughed. "Oh, you're so old-fashioned."

"Maybe I am, child, but it's the old-fashione
principles that keep one going in life. Remembe
that. I'd rather get to heaven in a horse and bugg
than wind up in hell going eighty miles an hou
down a highway."

Karen glanced quizzically at her aunt, trying t
sort out the message of her statement; but sh
shrugged giving up finally, as she always did
Aunt Ingrid mixed metaphors like she wa
inventing a new philosophy; but she meant well
bless her heart.

"Good-by. I must be leaving." Karen bent dow
and kissed her aunt. They clung together
moment; then Karen turned and walked to th
door, where the cab driver was waiting patiently

"You ready?" he asked. She nodded, and aske
him to bring the luggage from the bedroom; the
she walked outside, followed by Aunt Ingrid, wh
stood to one side on the stone pathway leadin
down to the garden gate, watching sadly as th
suitcases were loaded into the trunk of the taxi.

Karen gave her another hug, kissed her onc
more, and climbed into the back seat. Aunt Ingri
closed the garden gate, waving until the tax
disappeared around the corner of the street.

"O'Hare?" the driver asked.

"Yes. TWA terminal." Karen looked at he
watch. "We've got almost two hours."

"Good. I won't risk a speeding ticket, then."
The driver laughed and turned his head quickly
"You getting the London flight?"

"Yes."

"You'll enjoy it. My wife and I went over las

year. This your first trip abroad?"

Karen nodded. "Yes. I'm moving to Sweden to live. And go to school," she added.

"Hey, that's wonderful. You got relatives over there?"

"S'matter of fact, I do. What made you ask that?"

The driver grinned. "You said Sweden. And you look very Swedish. In fact, you're the Swedish looking passenger I've had all day." He chuckled at his outrageous pun, and Karen smiled pleasantly. "I've got an aunt in Scotland. My wife comes from Edinburgh. That's why we went over last year. We took a car at Heath Row and drove all the way up. That sure is beautiful country, especially when you get into the Scottish highlands."

"So I've heard."

"You should try it sometime. You'll enjoy it. The driving takes a little practice, though. Those crazy English. They drive on the wrong side of the road."

Karen laughed. "I bet that's what they say about us."

"I s'pose so."

She relaxed into the cushions and let her eyes linger on the passing traffic, growing dense as they approached the expressway.

"I'm sure glad you've got plenty of time," the driver observed. "This five o'clock traffic is murder."

"Yes. That's why I'm leaving early. I didn't want to get tied up and maybe miss the flight."

"Don't you worry. I'll get there in plenty of time."

Despite the driver's assurances, they pulled up

at O'Hare Airport at six-thirty. Karen glanced anxiously at her wrist watch. The driver saw her expression.

"Don't panic," he said cheerfully. "They won't take off without you."

He unloaded the luggage into the hands of a waiting skycap, and Karen hurried to the TWA counter, checked in and managed to arrive at the departure gate with almost forty-five minutes to spare. She collapsed into a chair, breathing a sigh of relief.

She looked around at her fellow passengers, an assortment of businessmen in suits, carrying attache cases; families en route to England and an early summer vacation; a few single women; and, Karen noticed with a flicker of interest, several single men. She wondered who would be seated next to her, and whether it could be one of the young men. Perhaps *that* one, she thought, fixing her gaze on a tall, dark-haired man reading a magazine casually, lifting his eyes now and then to glance at the jostling mass of humanity that was rapidly filling up the departure lounge. He turned his head and his eyes met Karen's. She looked down at once, feeling a little self-conscious at having been caught staring at him. She looked up again and saw he was still looking at her, a soft smile on his handsome features. She smiled back, then looked down again, her heart giving a jump. Stop it! This is no time to flirt, she reminded herself. Or was it? She had never really flirted in her life, except with Kevin, and that was years ago when she was an impressionable teenager, caught up in the mystique of the adolescent mating games played in high school.

Now she was a poised young woman, about to

embark on a new chapter in her life. So why shouldn't it include some exposure to the adult world of inter-acting relationships? The young man could easily be a very charming individual. If nothing else, he could help fill the span of hours on the plane. And, she thought with a twinge of excitement, he could very well be going on to Stockholm, like she was. Ridiculous! She examined him again out of the corner of her eye, and decided he was a graduate student, on his way to continue schooling at Oxford or Cambridge. He couldn't be more than twenty-two or three, she thought, and there was a rather academic look about him...

At that moment, he glanced towards the ticket counter and stood up quickly as a young woman approached him from the entrance to the lounge, pushing her way excitedly through the crowd, and flinging her arms around him. They kissed, almost too indiscreetly, Karen thought, for a public place; then they sat down, holding hands and staring into eachother's eyes with obvious adoration. Karen noticed a very new, very shiny wedding ring on the girl's left hand. So that took care of that! she thought wryly. A honeymoon couple, off to England for two weeks bliss...

She grinned to herself; then her pulses began racing as the loudspeaker crackled and a man's voice blasted above the murmur of conversations. "TWA Flight 770 for London is now ready for boarding..."

Karen stood up, clutched her handbag and her travel case and joined the throng that moved in a sedate stampede towards the exit door leading to the aircraft. Through the window she saw the Jumbo Jet waiting for the hundreds of passengers to pour into its cavernous interior. She felt a thrill of excitement prickle her nerves and she smiled happily. At last she was on her way, to a new world, to a new life. She wondered what lay ahead...and who was waiting somewhere to become part of that new life.

CHAPTER 2

The flight to London was uneventful. Karen was seated next to a corpulent, middle-aged businessman who, after a few desultory attempts at conversation, retreated behind a copy of TIME magazine and eventually fell asleep. After dinner, Karen fully intended to watch the movie, but unaccountably, she felt desperately sleepy. She leaned back, closed her eyes and awakened with a shock to discover they were about to land at Heath Row. The stewardess brought her a quick cup of coffee and a roll, grinning broadly and commenting on Karen's ability to sleep so soundly. "I tried to wake you for food," she said, "but you were out for the count. At least you won't suffer much from jetlag."

Karen stared out the window, fully awake now and eager to catch a glimpse of England for the first time; but low fog shrouded the ground, and she relaxed once again, disappointed, in her seat. She filled in her landing card and prepared herself to disembark.

The 747 touched down with barely a bump, taxied to the terminal and came to a stop. Slowly the passengers began filing off the plane in what seemed to Karen an endless, painfully slow procession. At last, she reached the door and was about to step out when her heel caught in the ridge between the aircraft floor and the connecting tube to the terminal; she gasped and felt herself pitching forward; then a strong hand seized her arm and pulled her up again. She swung around and looked into a young, handsome face that was grin-ning at her, the pale blue eyes staring mockingly into her own.

"Thank you so much," she said shakily.

"My pleasure," murmured the young man. "Next time perhaps you'd better leave those high heels at home." His tone was quite condescending and Karen flushed with embarrassment.

"I didn't realize..." she began, but he moved forward, his hand on her elbow, guiding her up the slight incline and into the terminal. She felt like a child being led by an angry parent and instinctively, she shook loose her arm, raised her chin defiantly and quickened her pace.

"I can manage very well now," she said crisply.

"Go ahead, then," he replied. "I'll follow, just in case you fall on your face again." His glance was mocking and his voice seemed to be purposefully irritating. Karen glared at him and marched forward, intending to ignore him completely. She appreciated his help, admittedly, but why did he have to be so superior about it? Probably one of those male chauvinist characters, she surmised. She'd show him! She was quite able to take care of herself, high heels and all...

They passed through customs and into the main reception area. Karen looked around, impressed by the modern magnificence of the terminal, with its shops, offices and eating places, all with clear, uncluttered signs and a total lack of the razzle-dazzle that characterized many American airports. But then, she reminded herself: this is England. Land of restraint and discretion. But she liked it. There was a curious dignity, an aura of quiet efficiency about the terminal that pleased her.

She looked around and breathed a sigh of relief. The young man had disappeared. Thank goodness! She felt if he had said one more word to her, she would have blown up and made a scene. She sighed gratefully, smiled to herself and began walking towards the restaurant. Missing the one meal on the plane had left her hungry, and she decided to stand herself a large, English-style dinner. Or should it be called breakfast? She realized it was 9:15 in the morning. A large, English-style breakfast, then, she thought: eggs, sausage, bacon—the works! Or didn't the English eat kippers for breakfast? She remembered her parents talking once about the English habit of having a steamed kipper to start the day. Well, perhaps it might be fun to try one, although the thought of anything fishy at this hour gave her a faintly queasy feeling.

She entered the restaurant, and was greeted at once by a smiling hostess, who seated her at a small table in the corner. Karen slipped off her coat, leaned back and studied the menu. Sure enough, kippers were listed!

The waitress approached, pad in hand and pencil poised in readiness. "Whatcha havin', duckie?" the woman asked in a distinct Cockney accent that brought an immediate smile to Karen's lips.

"This is my first trip over here," she confessed. "I'm going to try one of your kippers. Are they good?"

The waitress, a stocky woman in her late forties, shrugged her ample shoulders and grinned amiably. "They're good," she replied, "if you like 'em, that is. Tell you what, dearie. I'll bring you one, and if you can't stomach it, I'll take it back and bring you eggs and bacon. How's that for service?"

"Wonderful. You're awfully nice, thank you."

"And you bein' an American, which I can tell from that voice," the waitress continued breezily, "I s'pect you'll want coffee? Or maybe you want to try some tea? English style, that is, you know, with milk and sugar."

"That sounds good," said Karen, feeling suddenly very much at home and at ease with her surroundings. "You drink it like that all the time over here, don't you?"

"Sure do, duckie. It's the only thing to settle the nerves, calm the stomach and keep you regular."

Karen burst out laughing. "I like that," she said. "The only time we drink it that way in the States is if we're sick. My mother would always have tea whenever she felt bad."

The waitress chuckled. "We drink it all the time," she said. "Mebbe that's what keeps us from getting sick, wouldn't you say?" She dissolved in a great guffaw, and waddled back towards the counter.

Karen stared around the restaurant, which was fairly crowded, and through the windows she saw hundreds of passengers making their way to and fro along the concourse. Yet, for some reason, the people seemed to lack the desperate haste that was always apparent on the faces of air travelers back home. However, not all those people were English, she realized. There were probably representatives from every country in the world passing through Heath Row every hour. Maybe it was the British atmosphere that did it, Karen decided. There was, she felt, a definite something in the air that precluded any public display of emotion. No, wrong again! Over there in a corner of the restaurant she saw the honeymoon couple, squeezed into a booth and obviously holding hands under the table, staring into each other's eyes...

" 'Ere you are. A cuppa to get you going, and one big kipper."

Karen looked up as the waitress deposited her breakfast on the table with studied care.

"That...that's a kipper?" she said faintly, wrinkling her nose as the odor wafted up. The waitress dissolved into giggles.

" 'Old yer nose and take a bite. It's delicious."

"You'd better wait," said Karen bravely. "I don't know...it's not exactly what I thought it would be." She stared at the dark wrinkled object on the plate and picked up a fork.

"Look, dearie. Scrape the skin off. Yes, that's right. Now, take a bite of that lovely looking meat. Go on, don't be scared. It's good, and that's the honest-to-Gawd truth!"

Karen closed her eyes, and chewed slowly. Then she opened her eyes wide, and she nodded with delight. She swallowed, and beamed at the waitress.

"It's wonderful!" she said enthusiastically. "Oh, I'm going to enjoy this."

"Good. If you want anything else, I'll be right over there. Just give me a wave."

Karen settled down, her hunger sparked by the salty, tingling taste of the kipper. It reminded her of anchovies, or sardines, but slightly different, with a rich, meaty flavor. She was busily engaged in demolishing the kipper, and had almost finished, when she heard a soft chuckle at her elbow. She looked up to see, standing beside her table, the young man who had walked off the plane with her. He was smiling down at her, that same look of tolerant amusement on his face.

"Well, for an American, you've latched on to English habits very quickly," he commented.

"It's delicious," she replied.

"I know," he said. "We eat them in Sweden all the time."

Karen stared disbelievingly at him. "You...you're from Sweden?" she asked in a tight voice. "That's where I'm going. Stockholm."

"The noon flight to Arlanda?" he asked, and she nodded. "My, what a coincidence. I am, too. I say, would you mind if I joined you?"

"No, help yourself," said Karen, and he slid into the seat opposite her. Her former antagonism evaporated beneath the warmth of his voice. "My name's Lars Tengborn," he said. "Who are you?"

"Karen Christensen."

"Oh, then you're Swedish, too?"

Karen nodded. "Yes, my father came from Stockholm years ago. I was born in the States, though. Minnesota."

Lars grinned, and Karen noted that this time there was no hint of superiority, no mockery in his smile; just frank, honest expression of pleasure. She realized with a shock how terribly good-looking he was: tall, broad-shouldered but with sensitive, aesthetic features. And, she noted, that typical Swedish bloom in his cheeks, tanned, smooth but with a hint of color on the cheekbones. He looked like a most refined, cultured young gentleman. Yes, a gentleman, to be sure, she knew: something she had never recognized in any of the young men at school, and certainly not in Kevin, way back in high school. Was this perhaps just a quality inherent in Europeans, she wondered...?

"Minnesota? The little Sweden of America, or so I've been told. I've never been there."

"But you flew over on the same plane with me?"

"True, but I was merely visiting Chicago. I'm an industrial designer. I was having a conference with a big American company that's interested in some of my work."

"An industrial designer? That sounds very impressive. What do you design?"

"Machinery. Office equipment. All sorts of very dull things, really. Or I imagine you'd consider them dull."

"Not at all. I think that's wonderful. I've never met an industrial designer before, although a couple of kids at school were studying it, I remember."

"School?"

"Yes. Northwestern University in Chicago. I went there for one semester."

"Studying what?"

"Anthropology. I hope that doesn't frighten you," Karen added impishly, taking a last bite of her kipper and leaning back, sipping her tea.

"Not a bit. One of my good friends in

Stockholm is an anthropologist. He lectures at the University at Uppsala."

"That's where my uncle teaches."

"Oh. What's his name? Maybe I know him. I went to school there myself," Lars added quickly.

"Niels Christensen."

Lars beamed across the table. "Of course. I took a humanities course with him. A wonderful man. Very inspiring. Then you're going to visit him, no doubt?"

Karen nodded. "Not to visit. To live. And finish my degree at the university."

"How interesting. But when you say 'to live', does that mean you don't intend returning to America?"

"Not for a long time," said Karen. "You see..." She hesitated, realizing that this would be the first time she would have to explain what had happened to someone; to mention the fact that... "Well, my parents were killed six months ago," she managed to blurt out. "An avalanche in Switzerland."

Lars' face showed genuine regret. "I am sorry," he murmured.

"It's all right. I'm over it now," said Karen, feeling a rush of relief at realizing that she had been able to relate the tragic event without dissolving into tears. She *was* over it...

"And you have no other family in the States?"

"Only a maiden aunt in Chicago. And I couldn't see living with her. Actually, I felt I just wanted a complete change. Uncle Niels wrote and asked me to come to live with him, so I accepted."

"He is a wonderful man." Lars nodded. "You'll undoubtedly be very happy with him."

"I hope so. He's all I've got left in the world.

Except for Aunt Ingrid in Chicago, and...well, she's sweet and kind, but not the sort of woman I could ever feel really close to. I do feel close to Uncle Niels, even though I haven't seen him in ten years."

"So he'll be sending you through school, then?"

Karen shook her head quickly. "Oh, no. I..." She paused and blushed. "Well, you see, my parents were quite well off. I...I am able to take care of myself. Very well, in fact."

"I see." Lars leaned back, reached for a cigarette and lit up. "Oh, excuse me. You don't mind if I smoke?" he asked, and Karen shook her head. "Well, you have quite a future ahead of you, I'd say."

Karen smiled. "Yes, and it's all new and very exciting. In fact, that was my first trip on the jumbo jet, and my first visit to Europe. Or England, right now," she added with a little laugh. "I'm loving every minute of it, so far."

"And you'll continue," Lars said firmly. "You'll definitely love Sweden. It's the most beautiful country in the world."

Karen laughed softly. "That's understandable," she said.

"No, I mean it. And I've traveled extensively, too. Certainly every country has its good points. But I happen to think the Scandinavian countries have the best blend of everything. The summers are warm and you can swim and sunbathe. The winters are cold, icy and snowy—good weather for winter sports. You like to ski, by the way?"

"Love it,' replied Karen.

"Good. I'll have to take you skiing this winter. I know some of the best slopes." He took a drag off his cigarette and leaned forward eagerly.

"Anyway, as I was saying, I think Sweden has the best climate. Not only weather-wise, but for people. I think the drastic changes in the seasons breed a special quality in everyone. We are able to withstand adversity much better, and we are able to enjoy the good things with a greater degree of pleasure. Perhaps you've heard that we are notorious for being a very sensual race of people. We feel things more strongly, if you understand."

Karen nodded. "My father used to talk a lot about Sweden. He always said he wanted me to come back here. Not come back. I mean, visit. And I almost came with him and mother three years ago, but I decided not to. I had a summer planned in New Mexico, digging, and as I got credit for it, I felt I'd postpone the trip to Sweden." Her voice caught in her throat, and she looked away for a second, realizing that by putting off that trip, she ended any European trip with her parents forever. "I'm sorry, Lars," she continued, her voice firming again. "I was just thinking..."

"Your father? Don't, if it upsets you. I lost my father about ten years ago. I grieved for a long time until I realized it is senseless to grieve. We should remember the happy tmes we spend with certain people, and not wish for something that can never be. We must live in the present, not in the past."

Karen nodded. "True. And right now, I'm enjoying the present very much. Including talking to you, Lars. My, but I am rattling on, aren't I? But then, you're easy to talk to. You know that, of course?"

Lars dropped his eyes and for the first time, Karen saw a hint of self-consciousness in his expression. "I like people," he replied quietly. "Which is perhaps why I am able to talk to just about anybody without any qualms. I might say, however, that you are very easy to talk to yourself. And very easy to look at, may I add?"

"All right, that's enough!" Karen stared at him mischievously. "If you start flattering me, I'll just get up and leave."

"I wouldn't want that. I promise I'll try to ignore the fact that you're beautiful and very appealing..."

"I said that's enough, Lars!" Karen's voice held the barest suspicion of irritation, and he smiled at once, reaching over the table and squeezing her arm gently.

"Forgive me, Karen, please."

"You're forgiven."

"Good. I do want us to be friends. Especially as I know your uncle. I may come and visit you after you're settled in?"

"Of course."

"I'd like to show you around. Not only Stockholm and Uppsala, but all the other beautiful places in our country. You have no idea what a paradise it is. And if you're interested in anthropology, you'll enjoy it even more. The old castles. The historical places. Sweden is the perfect place for anyone interested in history."

"Good. I'll look forward to that." Karen hesitated a moment, unsure whether to pursue a question that had been balancing on the edge of her mind for minutes; finally she decided to go ahead. "I presume," she continued guardedly, "that you're single?"

Lars nodded and gave her a broad smile. "If I were a married man, do you think I'd be paying you those compliments a moment ago?"

"Yes. I've had many passes from married men,"

Karen lied smoothly. "They're the ones you have to watch out for," she added with a coy giggle.

"Where I come from," said Lars playfully. "It's the single men you have to watch out for. We have very liberal attitudes towards relationships in Scandinavia, in case you haven't heard. A man and a woman will live together for a while before getting married, just to make sure they're suited. I think it's an excellent idea, although some foreigners think we are very immoral."

"Oh. Then perhaps I should have asked whether you live alone," said Karen, her eyes twinkling merrily.

"I do." Lars met her gaze without any hesitation or reluctance. "I happen to believe that one can have a passing affair, but if you're going to live together, you should be married."

"How odd, considering what you just said. You obviously don't go along with the rest of the country, then?"

Lars shook his head. "No, I have rather tradtional attitudes, I'm afraid." He pursed his lips. "I guess that's my father's influence," he said wryly.

"With me, it was my mother," Karen said softly, and the words were out before she realized it. She flushed and took a sip of tea to hide her passing confusion. Lars noticed her expression and he nodded understandingly.

"If you're trying to say what I think you are," he said, "You have my profoundest admiration. It is a lucky man today who gets a virgin for his wife."

"Oh, Lars, please!" Karen looked down at her cup awkwardly. "You're embarrassing me now."

"I'm sorry. Perhaps we should have some more tea. In fact, I'd like to order something to eat myself." He raised his hand and beckoned the waitress, who waddled over knowingly and stood, staring down at them both.

"My, my, duckie, ain't he a handsome one?" she said explosively. "He ain't your husband, is he?"

"Oh, dear, this is getting worse," said Karen, and then suddenly her embarrassment evaporated and she dissolved into the giggles. "No, we've just met."

Lars eyed her speculatively. "Why?" he asked the waitress. "Do you think we make a good couple?"

"You certainly do," was the reply. "And if I were you, I'd do something about it."

"Well, right now I'd like you to do something about some more tea for the young lady," said Lars, stifling a grin, "and I'd like some eggs and bacon, with white toast, please."

"Be right back," said the waitress, moving away to the service counter.

Karen managed to stop giggling and stared at Lars for a moment. "You're too much," she murmured. "But I do like you. I'm glad we met, even though it was under odd circumstances. I mean, my falling as I came out the plane. It's lucky you were there."

"It was fate." Lars' eyes twinkled humorously. "Maybe I'm the one who fell, really. I can never resist a pretty face."

"There you go again." Karen pouted in pretended anger. "We've only just met."

"True, but I feel I've known you all my life."

They stared at each other, and Karen felt a warm glow permeate her body. He was so attractive, and his manner charming to the extreme. So different from the way she felt about him after his initial brush with her getting off the plane.

Maybe it was fate, she thought; maybe Lars Tengborn is the man who's been waiting to become part of my life. He's handsome, and talented, and obviously well-to-do. Industrial designing paid well, she knew. And if she was going to become involved with a man, it would have to be someone well-off, she had decided months ago; if not, she would always have the nagging suspicion that he was only after her because of her money. It would be interesting to see how their relationship developed. All of a sudden, she felt hungry again.

"I think I'll have some eggs as well," Karen said.

Lars raised his hand and gave the order to the waitress. He looked across the table and smiled tenderly at her. "That's a good sign," he said, and there was that old hint of mockery in his voice again, very faintly, but it was there.

"Why?" asked Karen curiously.

Lars chuckled. "I took two years of psychology," he replied carefully. "And I distinctly remember something about a woman getting hungry when she can't satisfy another desire that she feels."

Karen stared at him speechlessly. "I think that's awful," she finally managed to say. "And very presumptuous of you, too, I might add."

"You mean it's not true?"

"Certainly not."

"I thought you liked me."

"I do, but that doesn't mean I'm panting to go to bed with you."

Lars colored slightly. "Put as bluntly as that," he said stiffly. "It takes all the romance away."

"There's nothing romantic in what you said."

"Come on, I was only joking. Where's your sense of humor?"

"You weren't joking, and you know it."

"I just said I was."

"Well, I don't think you were. And I don't appreciate it one bit." Karen suddenly realized her voice was getting louder and more angry each second, but, she felt, he deserved it. "So let's keep the conversation general from now on."

"Very well, whatever you say," Lars replied coldly, and at that moment, the waitress arrived at the table with their food. She put the plates down and stood a moment, eyeing them both. Then she chuckled. "My, my," she observed. "You've just met and you're having a good old knock-down-drag-out already. Must be love, that's all I can say, dearies." And before Karen or Lars could respond, she turned and marched back to the kitchen, laughing to herself.

Lars looked at Karen and began to smile. Karen kept a straight face as long as she could; then she, too, felt herself mellow as her anger left her, and her face relaxed into a smile.

"I don't think either of us should say anything more until we've finished our meal," Lars said in a very matter-of-fact tone.

Karen nodded. "I agree," she replied, and they both began eating, but every few seconds, their eyes met and Karen read more in his glance than he could ever have said in words.

CHAPTER 3

The SAS 727 jetliner had made the final turn and began its descent into the Arlanda Airport. Karen stared excitedly out of the window, her eyes straining for a glimpse of the city. "I can't see much," she complained, and Lars laughed understandingly.

"We're miles from Stockholm," he explained. "Arlanda was built to handle the international traffic, and was put way out to avoid flying over the built-up areas. If you take a domestic flight, you'll land at the old one—Bromma—which is only six miles from Stockholm. Then you'll see something of the city, but not here. The country is beautiful, though," he added consolingly. "Maybe one day I can take you for a flight in a small plane. You'll see a lot then."

Karen shook her head. "That's all right," she answered. "I'll stick to the jets. I feel they're safer."

"You should, though. Stockholm from the air is impressive, with the blend of modern buildings side-by-side with the old traditional Swedish architecture. And," he added, "if you come and visit me in my office, you'll get a good view of what I mean."

"You're high up?" asked Karen.

"Yes. On the 14th floor, to be exact. The Wenner-Gren Administrative Center is a new building, very modern. Almost too modern, really. It has no style to it. Just a tall black and gray rectangle towering over the city, and right below, on each side of the street, are some of the oldest apartment houses in Stockholm. The contrast is quite spectacular."

Karen nodded. "I can picture that," she murmured. "In most American cities, the new buildings are like that: functional but not very beautiful. I've always preferred a building to have some character to it. I think it's sad that progress seems to rule out the beauty that used to exist in architecture."

"It's a matter of economy," Lars explained. "Centuries ago, artisians could afford to spend years on putting those special touches like they did on Notre Dame Cathedral and similar places. Today, a building is put up purely to satisfy the need for working space. it has to be built as cheaply as possible, with the most practical use of floor space. I know only too well. That's part of my philosophy in industrial design."

"You must feel somewhat stifled creatively, or aren't you that concerned with aesthetics?" asked Karen.

"No, I manage a happy compromise," he replied with a laugh. "Of course, I sometimes wind up having to fight for my designs, but then, that's part of the game. We have to fight for everything we believe in these days. Corporate industry is truly a ratrace. Survival of the shrewdest."

"Or survival of those with the strongest nerves, eh?" Karen chuckled. "I remember daddy used to complain about that. He said he wished things could be like they were thirty years ago, when a man's word was his bond, and business was done with more honesty."

Lars nodded. "The whole world is changing," he said. "And I'm not sure if it's for the better. People are becoming too greedy, too interested in making money instead of making themselves happy."

"True. But then, often we have to have money to afford the things that make us happy."

Lars snorted. "Anyone who relies on things for his happiness is chasing his own tail," he said forcefully. "It's one's deeper sense of spiritual values that really brings us ultimate contentment."

Karen chuckled. "Now you sound like my father." She looked at him quizzically. "But then, you've already indicated you're a bit old-fashioned in your outlook. Not that it's a detriment," she added hastily, noticing a slight frown creep across his face. "I'd much rather someone held on to traditional values. They're a much firmer foundation for character than most of today's uncaring attitudes."

Lars smiled indulgently. "My, my, you're quite a philosopher, aren't you?" He laughed softly. "But I like that. In fact, I'm beginning to realize there's a lot about you I like very much, Karen." His eyes were warm as they met hers, and she nodded agreement.

"I like you, too, Lars," she murmured, and their conversation came to a close as the plane touched the ground and the pilot reversed the engines, slowing the aircraft down with a massive shuddering that precluded any further talking until they reached the confines of the terminal. Which was just as well, Karen thought: she preferred, at this point in their relationship, to keep things general, and away from personal aspects of their feelings for each other.

She liked Lars, she admitted; in fact, she liked him very much. He seemed an ideal young man—intelligent, considerate, good looking—but she didn't want him to jump to any conclusions about her. She would go out with him; in fact, she was eagerly looking forward to exploring Stockholm with him. But only as friends; nothing more serious, not for the moment. She felt very comfortable with him. They seemed to blend beautifully, except when his surface superiority was allowed to assert itself and he assumed that irritatingly condescending tone of voice; but then, she rationalized, she probably had a few qualities that could stand improvement. No one is perfect, and at least Lars came closest to the type of young man she hoped she might meet one day. And she felt quite grateful they had met, because now she had one new friend in the new land she intended making her home.

They passed through customs, picked up their baggage and made their way to the sidewalk outside the front of the terminal. Karen looked about, searching for Uncle Niels, remembering him vaguely from memory, but more specifically from a picture he had sent her recently: of him outside his home in Uppsala, leaning against the waist-high stone wall surrounding the old farmhouse, his medium-length gray hair blowing in the breeze, and an irresistible smile on his clean-shaven face. Not unlike her own father, Karen had thought when she first saw the picture, but a little younger, a litle thinner; but they had the same large twinkling eyes.

"See him?" Lars asked, and Karen shook her head.

"I can't imagine what's happened." Her voice sounded fretful and anxious. "He said his last class was at eleven. And it's now after three. He should have been here in plenty of time. Unless he had an accident, of course."

"Maybe something's come up. Why not check at the SAS counter? There might be a message for you."

Karen's face brightened. "Now why didn't I think of that?"

"Because you're a scatter-brained young lady, that's why," Lars replied mischievously. "A typical American girl. Right?"

"Wrong," she said quickly. "I'm very level-headed and I'm not one of those terrible females you've seen in Hollywood movies. So there. Come on, let's go check at the counter."

They turned, forcing their way through the crush of people and made their way back down the concourse to the SAS counter. Karen enquired of the clerk, who shook his head regretfully. "No message," he told her, "but if we get one, you should hear the announcement over the loudspeakers."

"Thank you very much."

"Now what?" said Lars. "Are you going to wait for him?"

"I don't think so. He would certainly have been here by now. I think I'll call him. I have his home phone number with me in my purse."

They hurried to a nearby phone booth and Karen placed a collect call to Niels Christensen in Uppsala. Lars stood by, grinning knowingly. "You've got a long wait," he murmured. "Our phone system isn't the best in the world."

"I've got plenty of time," Karen retorted pleasantly.

Fifteen minutes passed before the call was completed, and the operator informed Karen there was no answer at the number. She hung up, stepped outside the booth and faced Lars hopelessly. "No answer," she said in answer to his unspoken question.

"All right. There's only one thing left to do," he said, taking her arm firmly and leading her towards the entrance. "I'll drive you to Uppsala."

"Oh, no, I couldn't let you do that," Karen protested. "I can take a taxi."

"You must be wealthy," he said, grinning. "No, it will be no trouble at all. Besides, I want to make sure you get there safe and sound."

"I can take care of myself. Stop treating me like a child."

"If you were a child, young lady," Lars said humorously, "I wouldn't even have talked to you in the first place. And I'm only treating you with some Scandinavian hospitality, so don't refuse me."

"Well..." Karen hesitated, then she smiled gratefully. "I do appreciate it, Lars."

"My pleasure." They paused at the edge of the sidewalk, and Lars beckoned the porter to follow them with the luggage. "My car's parked over there," he said indicating the massive parking lot that stretched, it seemed, limitlessly ahead of them. "I left it here last week when I flew to Chicago."

They made their way up the long ramp, and about a hundred yards ahead, parked in a corner, was a gleaming new yellow Volvo station wagon. The porter loaded their baggage, and Karen climbed in the passenger seat, feeling suddenly very excited and filled with anticipation now that the final leg of her long journey was beginning; and she could think of no one nicer (except Uncle Niels, of course!) to drive her to her new home.

Lars slid behind the wheel, guided the car carefully through the winding exit ramps on to the highway, crammed with cars. Karen stared around, wide-eyed, drinking in the scenery, the broad freeways and the modern appearance of the terminal area. "My, this could be any major American airport," she gasped. "The cars, and the roads...everything. I feel completely at home already."

"Good." Lars glanced at her affectionately. "That's the way we want everyone to feel when they come to Sweden. And the longer you stay, the better you'll enjoy it, I know. There have been many students come to study here, and wind up never going back to America."

Karen snuggled back against the comfortable leather seat, and sighed contentedly. "I'll go back one day," she said quietly.

"I'm sure you will, but I have a feeling you're going to make Sweden your home from now on."

"That's my intention. There's really nothing to go back to America for, except to see it again, of course."

"What about your aunt in Chicago?"

Karen shrugged. "She said she might come over here and visit. Though I doubt it." She giggled at the memory of Aunt Ingrid's face. "She said she'd have to come by ship. She's terrified of flying."

Lars nodded. "I don't blame her. A lot of people are. And a sea voyage is great. You've never taken one?"

Karen shook her head. "No, never."

"You must. There are many excursions by ship which you would enjoy, right here in Scandinavia, especially up the fjords."

"Oh, yes, of course. I'm planning to see those. Daddy took some pictures when he and my mother came over a few years ago. He told me they are unbelievably beautiful."

Lars nodded "The Sogne Fjord in Norway is fantastic. It cuts 112 miles into the mountains. When you travel up by ship, you pass under these massive rocky cliffs, almost 5000 feet high, right up near the Jostedalsbreen glacier, which is the largest in Europe. I went there once after I graduated from high school. I've never forgotten it. I felt so insignificant, so unimportant. In fact, whenever I get depressed about anything, especially in my work, I remember that glacier, and the thousands of years it took to form it. Things like that make one realize that no matter what our problems may be, or how serious we consider a situation, the world will continue, as it always has, as it always will."

Karen nodded, impressed by the sudden seriousness in his voice. "You're a deep person, aren't you, Lars?"

He laughed self-consciously. "Only sometimes. But then, I like to balance my life. It can't be all fun, games, disco dancing and drinking and all that. To be honest, I enjoy staying home and curling up by the fire with a good book. In winter, that's about all I do at night, really."

"No girl-friend?" Karen asked, trying to keep her voice as light as possible.

He shook his head. "I went with one girl about a year ago, but we broke up. She thought I was too stuffy," he added, grinning.

"And you? Do you think you're stuffy?"

"No. I think I'm a rather well-balanced individual, if you must know. I can go out and have a ball with the best of them, but I'm just as comfortable alone, at home, studying, or reading, listening to good music. I get most of my inspiration for my work, alone, with Beethoven or Mozart on the stereo."

"It sounds like you don't really have much time for a girl friend," said Karen.

"I have the time, but unless a girl can enjoy the same things I do, I lose interest very quickly. Life is for sharing, I feel, and how can you share your life with someone who couldn't care less about the things you like?"

"True. That's been my problem with boy-friends. I can never find one who can talk about anything but rock music, dancing or making out. I do like to go out and have fun, but, like you said, I much prefer someone who can have a serious discussion now and then."

Lars nodded, taking his eyes off the road for a second to look at her appreciatively. "It sounds like we have a lot in common," he commented lightly. "You're really rather mature for somone so young."

"Not so young," Karen said quickly. "I'll be

twenty-one in a few months. A full-fledged adult."

Lars laughed. "A mere child," he said teasingly.

"Well, how old are you? Twenty-three...four?"

Lars burst out laughing again, shaking his head sadly. "Oh, how I only wish," he said. "No, Karen. I'm twenty-nine."

She gasped. "Wow! You sure don't look it."

"It's this beautiful climate," he replied. "It keeps us all young looking. You know what they say aout the Scandinavian stereotype—peaches and cream complexion, slender, firm bodies, long lifespan. People look better and live longer over here."

"Even with the modern rush of life today?" Karen waved her hand at the dense traffic on either side of them, and the cluster of buildings on one side of the freeway.

"Even with that. Remember, only a small percentage of people live in an urban area. The majority are in small towns, dotted around the country. We place a great stress on family life, on the old virtues, I guess you'd call it. We may have our modern trends and our liberal outlook towards sex, but deep down, we're really very solid, traditional people at heart."

"That's nice. I feel that way myself. I always have. Oooh.." She stretched her arms out in front of her and sighed happily. "I do believe I'm going to be very happy here."

"Good. I hope I can help you achieve some of that happiness," said Lars.

"That's a very provocative statement." Karen looked at him impishly, admiring his strong profile against the passing landscape. She had always liked strong noses and firm chins, she thought.

"Not provocative, just hopeful," Lars replied, glancing at her again quickly. "I haven't met a girl like you in years, Karen."

"That's not saying much for the girls over here."

"I mean it. Maybe it's because you're from another country, totally unused to things in Sweden. Until you settle down after a few years, you'll always have that naive charm that visitors exhibit—like a child with a new toy, eager to enjoy it every second. It's refreshing. Nothing turns me off quicker than a girl who pretends she's seen it all, knows it all and is bored with life. You know the type."

Karen smiled. "Yes, I've known people like that. It's sad, really. Every day there's always something new to excite one's interest, to keep one perking."

"And you're a very perky young lady, I might say. I'm going to have a lot of fun showing you around, I can see that now."

"Good. I think I'll enjoy that."

"I hope so. I plan to see a lot of you, Karen."

"Oh. What about your work?"

"I don't work all the time. And I rarely take work home, like some of the men at the Center. I feel if I put in eight hours at my desk. I've earned my money. I have evenings free, and weekends. In fact, perhaps I can come up to Uppsala next weekend and show you around. Would you like that?"

"Of course. I'm sure Uncle Niels has an extra room, and if you took a course with him, he's going to enjoy seeing you again."

"Yes. I'm looking forward to seeing him again, too. Talking of that, I do hope he isn't on his way to Arlanda. He might have thought you were on a later flight, you know."

"I don't think so. I sent him all the details. No..." Karen sighed. "I imagine he's just got hung up somewhere. I told him if we missed each other, I'd find my way to his house."

"Good." Lars pointed to a sign at the roadside. 'We're halfway there," he said. "I told you it wouldn't take long." He glanced at her for a moment. "You're not hungry, are you? Would you like to stop for something to eat?"

Karen burst out laughing. "Good grief, no! After that enormous breakfast, and that sandwich on the plane, I'm stuffed. What about you, though?" She looked at him anxiously. "If you're hungry, we can stop."

He shook his head. "No, I'm fine."

"I'm sure Uncle Niels will have dinner ready when we get there," Karen said. "Perhaps you can stay and eat with us before driving back?"

"That sounds wonderful. Thank you."

"Uncle Niels has a girl-friend, name of Annabelle. She teaches English at the university. Daddy met her once, and says she's a barrel of fun. She's also a barrel," Karen added with a chuckle. "Fat, forty-ish and quite sweet, I believe."

"Oh. I wonder if that's Annabelle Simpson..."

"Yes. Simpson. That's her last name. I remember now."

Lars laughed. "I've met her, I believe. And she is a lot of fun. Why is it portly people always seem to enjoy themselves so much?"

"It's their nature," said Karen. "They say it isn't healthy to be fat, but most of those I know seem to get a lot more out of life than skinny types. My mother was a little on the plump side, and a very happy person. Her sister—my aunt Ingrid—is very thin and looks like the world's just come to an end. I really feel sorry for her. She's kind, terribly kind, but very old-maidish. It's a pity she never married."

Lars raised an eyebrow. "You believe marriage is a cure-all for humanity's ailments?"

"Not necessarily, but I do approve of it."

"Good. That's another thing we have in common."

They looked at each other for a moment, and Karen again felt that warm glow of pleasure at their unspoken agreement. Yes, she decided, she would definitely be seeing a lot of Lars Tengborn. The more they talked, the closer she felt to him. He was someone, she knew, she could rely on; someone to share her innermost secrets with; someone she could...dare she even think it?—someone to love? She turned away, staring back out the window, afraid to let her mind wander into areas that were not only premature, but a little frightening. She had never really been in love, apart from that thwarted infatuation with Kevin; yet was this feeling inside her the beginnings of love?

She had never really believed one could fall in love in a flash; yet it happened, she felt sure. But then, apart from a natural admiration of Lars' good looks, she had not really been overwhelmed by the sight of him as he caught her arm when she fell; and his remarks afterwards had been anything but endearing. It was only after he had sat down at the table in the restaurant at Heath Row that she began to realize how charming he was; how thoroughly likeable; and now, after hours of conversation, she felt she had known him all her life. And the more he told her about himself, the more she felt drawn to him. She had, several times since they met, wanted to reach out and touch his face, to feel the incredible smoothness of his skin beneath her fingers, to slide her arms around those broad shoulders of his...

Enough, she chastised herself! This was ridiculous. For all she knew,he could, despite his statements, only be interested in a passing affair. All this talk about being so reserved, so traditional in his attitudes, could be mere window dressing to allay her fears over his intentions. After all, he was almost ten years older than she was—ten years more experience with women, and here she was, a virginal innocent from Minneapolis, on her first trip abroad, and making no effort to conceal her naivete.

How was she to know he wasn't putting on a big front for her benefit, and then, at the appropriate moment, he might try to have his way with her? It could be. She remembered her mother's words some years ago: warning her about the devious nature of some men on the make. "They can be as warm and wonderful as can be until they get what they want, and then they don't even know you."

Karen turned back from the window and looked hard at Lars as he sat behind the wheel, steering the care carefully through the traffic. Was he for real? she wondered, or was he just putting on an act for her? As if sensing her thoughts, he turned for a moment and smiled at her.

"We're almost there," he said, and his rich, reassuring voice chased her doubts as quickly as they had arisen in her mind. No, Lars was no shallow opportunist, she decided. He was everything he had said he was, she knew. He had to be, because the way she felt about him, she couldn't bear it if he wasn't. Did this mean she was falling in love with him? Her heart beat quicker at the thought, and Karen turned back to watch the passing scenery, trying desperately to quell the urge to move across the seat and put her arm around him...

CHAPTER 4

The wide, flat countryside began to give way to farmhouses, then an occasional roadside cafe, and finally, to the outskirts of Uppsala. Lars had said he knew the university area, and that the address of Uncle Niels' home was not far from the campus. She had questioned this statement, remembering that she had always been under the impression her uncle lived out in the country.

Lars had chuckled. "The university is on the edge of town," he explained. "A mile from the dean's office is farmland. Not acres and acres of it, but tidy little lots with a farmhouse and enough land around it to keep a cow, maybe a couple of pigs. But definitely not suburbia as you think of it in the States."

"As long as you know where to go," Karen had said, and left it in his hands, and he had driven on, completely confident. Obviously there was little that could ruffle Lars' outwardly calm composure. Karen felt nervous, apprehensive, not only because of the fact that her uncle did not meet her as arranged, but because they would undoubtedly arrive unexpectedly. Or maybe Uncle Niels took it for granted she would make her way without any problems... It was a little disconcerting, and Karen was grateful for Lars taking over so firmly, with such self-assurance. She settled back and her concerns faded beneath her burgeoning interest in the buildings—all old, ivy-covered and reeking of an academic atmosphere. Had she not known it, she would easily have guessed that Uppsala was a university town. There had always been a certain air about a city with a center of learning—an aura of quiet dignity, gentle repose and inspiring atmosphere. She thrilled to the thought that she would be continuing her studies here, becoming a part of this age-old institution and sharing its warmth and its high standing. Uppsala was renowned throughout Europe for its top-flight instructors and its demanding curriculum. Students did not go to Uppsala to stage protest marches against vague causes halfway across the world, like so many American institutions of learning were plagued with; students at Uppsala went there to improve their education and take advantage of one of the most respected staffs of teachers anywhere in Europe.

Lars slowed down and stopped at a corner, staring up at the street signs. "I think this is where we turn," he murmured, almost to himself; then he spun the steering wheel and they moved around the bend on to a small, tree-lined avenue. Karen could see a house peeking through the trees, every hundred yards or possibly more. It was not congested with homes, like the area they had just passed through; but then, that had been the actual campus, where, she knew from her own experience at college, housing was at a premium and every available room was rented out to students; and every spare foot of land was covered by some form of dwelling, either apartments or dormitories. Here, obviously, they were heading out of town, towards the gloriously green countryside, alive with trees and flower gardens and, at the back of each house, enough pastureland to maintain livestock. She saw several cows behind a fence, and further down the road, a horse was galloping playfully across a small field.

The houses were delightful, and Karen estimated each one to be no less than fifty years old; possibly older. Many had thatched roofs, a practice born of necessity to keep out the cold during the severe winters. Most of them were single storey, too, she noticed, giving the structures a cozy, intimate appearance like little old English cottages. In the gathering twilight, Karen felt she was floating through a gossamer world of make-believe—a fairyland of picturesque houses out of which, at any moment, there might parade seven little dwarfs waving good-by to Snow White at the door... It was almost unreal, and Karen found herself becoming almost tearfully happy as they drove down the street slowly, with Lars searching for numbers on the small, white picket gates set in the middle of most front gardens, enclosed solidly with rough stone walls.

"This is it." The car pulled up and Karen recognized the place from the photographs Uncle Niels had sent her. Quaint and appealing as it had appeared in pictures, the house looked even more attractive, the light sending a welcome into the gathering dusk from the diamond-paned windows on each side of the front door.

She turned to Lars. "I can hardly believe it," she whispered. "I'm here at last." Her lips quivered and Lars saw the tears in her eyes. "All right, let's not ruin your makeup," he said teasingly, opening the door and getting out quickly. "Come on, let's go see who's at home." He glanced towards the house. "Obviously someone's there. I can see a figure moving about."

His brusqueness chased Karen's pending attack

of sentiment, and she raised her chin, sniffed quickly and got out of the car. She smiled, feeling once more in control of herself, and took Lars' arm. Together they walked through the gate and up the narrow pathway, edged with roses. As they reached the front door, it swung open and, silhouetted against the lights inside, Karen saw a plump figure in an apron, her hair wisping around her eyes and her hands extended in a broad welcome.

"It must be Karen," said Annabelle Simpson, her voice exuding warmth and happiness. "How good to see you, child. I'm Annabelle. Niels has probably told you about me. Come in, come in."

'Hello," said Karen. "This is Lars Tengborn. He was good enough to drive me here. Uncle Niels never showed at the airport."

Annabelle shook Lars' hand, gave him a close scrutiny, grinned, and then led the way into the small livingroom. "Of course your uncle never met you," she said boisterously. "He's been busy at the college. Didn't they give you the message?"

"What message?"

Annabelle shook her head disgustedly. "He called SAS about twelve o'clock. Told them to inform you he was busy, and to take a taxi." She chuckled. "He knew you'd be able to afford it, you young rich heiress," she added, putting her arm around Karen and hugging her affectionately. "My, but you're a pretty one. Much lovelier than your photographs, my dear."

"I think I'll go unload Karen's things," said Lars, moving to the door.

"Fine. I'd help you, only I have to watch the stove. I'm cooking dinner. You will stay, won't you?"

"Thank you, that would be nice," said Lars, and walked back out to the car, leaving Karen looking around the room, her mind reeling beneath the sheer overpowering homeliness of the place. She felt, in a sudden flash, that she *had* come home.

"What a lovely room," she murmured, letting her eyes stray over the beautiful hand-rubbed antique furniture, the bookshelves reaching to the ceiling, and the rich velvet drapes by the windows.

"I like it," said Annabelle. "You should have seen it before I got busy here. Niels isn't what you'd call artistic, so I decided I'd better do something. He grumbled a lot, but I had my way. I usually do," she finished with a self-satisfied smirl.

"Where is Uncle Niels?" asked Karen. "Still at school?"

"Goodness, no!" Annabelle broke into a raucous guffaw. "He's out back taking care of Millie. That's his pet cow, in case you don't know. She's had some problem with an udder. Quite embarrassing. I know I'd feel quite upset if a man began putting a bandage around my nipples, believe me. Poor Millie. I guess that idiot farmboy got too enthusiastic when he was milking her yesterday."

Karen grinned, noticing the devilish look in Annabelle's big, brown eyes. They stared at each other a moment, then Annabelle stepped forward and embraced her once more. "Oh, Niels is going to be so glad to see you," she said. "I'll call him." She released Karen, went through to the back door and stuck her head out. A moment later, the house echoed to her penetrating English tones. "Nieeeels! You've got company!" She turned and saw the amused expression on Karen's face. "Before I became educated and started teaching," she said. "I used to work on my father's farm in Yorkshire. I had to call the workmen in for lunch each day. They sometimes said they could hear me in the next county."

Karen was about to remark on the delicious smell coming from the stove, when she heard the thump of footsteps outside, and seconds later, Uncle Niels burst into the kitchen.

"Karen!"

"Uncle Niels!"

They embraced, holding each other close, and Karen's pentup emotions finally burst and streamed down her cheeks in a happy release.

"There, there, child, you're home now." Niels' rich voice held all the tenderness and comfort that Karen remembered from her father, and she wept, letting the final dregs of sorrow drain from her, leaving her not empty, but with an ultimate sense of relief. She dried her eyes and stood, staring at her uncle. He was exactly as she had pictured him from the photograph: stocky, narrow-waisted, with firm, muscular arms and a thick neck, and on his rugged features there was a look of such infinite understanding and love that Karen almost dissolved into tears again. Annabelle observed their meeting with a motherly smile on her plump features. She wiped her forehead clear of the strands of bright red hair that, Karen was to discover, were forever sagging into her eyes. "All right, you two," she said brightly, "why don't you go into the livingroom and settle down. I've got the sherry and glasses all ready there. Oh, Lars..." She looked up as Lars appeared in the doorway. "Have you unloaded everything?"

He nodded. "They're by the front door," he replied. "Where do they go?"

"I'll show you," said Annabelle, bustling forward and leaving Karen and her uncle alone in the kitchen, still staring at each other disbelievingly.

"Oh, it's so good to be here," Karen whispered. "I'm sorry I..."

"Not a word, my dear. It's been a trying time for you, I'm sure. I'm sorry I couldn't meet you, but I had an urgent faculty meeting. I presume this young man brought you...?" His eyes twinkled. "Who is he, may I ask?"

"I'm sorry. I should've introduced you. I will in a minute. His name's Lars Tengborn. He's an industrial designer. We met on the plane. He's just come back from Chicago."

"He seems very nice."

"He is. Terribly nice, Uncle Niels. And I'm so grateful he drove me up here. I didn't know what had happened. The airline never gave me your message."

"No matter." Niels brushed the matter aside. "You're here. That's all that counts. And Annabelle has a wonderful dinner just about ready, from the smell. And she is such a wonderful cook. Wonderful in every way, I might add." He looked at her speculatively. "I presume you know Annabelle and I are..." He raised his eyebrows meaningfully. Karen nodded.

"As long as two people make each other happy, I don't mind what their situation is," she said quickly. "Of course," she added, with a mischievous twinkle in her eyes, "if and when you two get married, I'd love to be a bridesmaid."

"Enough of that," said Niels gruffly. "But

between you and me, I think I may finally talk her into it. Annabelle is a most stubborn woman, I might add. I think she hates the idea of being pinned down permanently..." He looked up as the clatter of footsteps heralded Annabelle and Lars returning from putting the luggage in the bedroom. "Ah, there you are, my dear. I was just telling Karen you have something magical brewing on the stove."

"Yes, I do," said Annabelle briskly, moving across and peeking into a large copper saucepan. "We'll be eating in about ten minutes, which gives Karen time to wash up and relax. You, too, Lars. You saw where the bathroom is. Why don't you show Karen?"

"Yes, and I'll pour us some sherry," said Niels.

Five minutes later, they were seated in the livingroom, sipping sherry and listening to Annabelle's subdued mumbling to herself as she put the finishing touches to the meal on the kitchen table, a large ranch-style spread that extended completely across one end of the room, with hand-carved chairs on both sides, and an exquisite linen cloth on which pale blue china gleamed enticingly.

"Well, as you Americans say, come and get it."

Niels rose, drained his sherry glass quickly and extended his arm to Karen. "May I escort you in to dinner, my dear?" he said grandly, winking at Lars. "You won't mind, young man, will you?"

"Of course not." Lars grinned at the older man, and followed them into the kitchen, where Annabelle was poised, one hand on her hip, the other waving them to their seats.

"I'm English," she said, sounding like an announcer introducing contestants at a boxing match. "Niels is Swedish, as you are, Lars. And Karen is American. So I decided I'd have a truly international dinner. English roast beef, Yorkshire pudding, green beans and potatoes with lots of thick, delicious gravy. Swedish home-baked bread. And for dessert, a gelatin dessert, which I've been told, is very American. Don't you put gelatin over everything, including salads?"

"Sometimes," said Karen guardedly, her mouth watering as she sat down and observed the sumptuous spread on the table. "I'll show you one of my favorite salads one day. Shredded carrots, chopped green olives, thinly sliced zucchini, all molded in a green lime jello. It's fantastic, and so easy to fix."

"Sounds horrendous," muttered Annabelle, "but I'll be willing to give it a go. Come on, Niels, you carve the roast before it gets cold."

Niels picked up the carving knife and fork and attacked the meat with an experienced hand, slicing it thinly and serving each one in turn. They settled down to the meal, and Karen suddenly realized how hungry she was. By the time they had consumed the dessert, a delicious fruit compote set in strawberry gelatin, she felt relaxed and satisfied. Niels took out his pipe, and Annabelle and Lars lit cigarettes.

"Coffee will be ready in a minute," Annabelle said.

"This was fantastic." Karen smiled at the older woman appreciatively. "Do you do the cooking all the time for Uncle Niels?"

"Only on special occasions," Annabelle replied archly, "when he allows it. Besides, I don't want to spoil him."

"And this is a very special occasion, my dear."

Niels looked at Karen with a soft smile on his face. "I can't tell you how much I have been looking forward to this moment."

"Me, too, It's going to be very exciting, getting used to the new customs, to new friends. I've already made one." She looked at Lars, who was leaning back in his chair, observing her closely with a penetrating look. "If they're all as nice as Lars is, I know I'm going to enjoy it."

"And with those kind words ringing in my ears," said Lars, pushing his chair back, "I think I'd best be heading back to Stockholm."

"So soon? Aren't you waiting for coffee?" asked Annabelle.

"I'd better not," Lars said regretfully. "It's going to be quite late when I get home, and I have some paperwork to take care of before going into the office in the morning."

"You will come back, won't you?" asked Niels.

"Of course. In fact..."

"Oh, yes. This weekend." Karen interrupted him quickly. "I wonder, Uncle Niels..." She turned to him imploringly. "Would it be all right if Lars came up and stayed here? you have room?"

"I'd be delighted," said Niels. "Whatever Karen wants is fine with me. This is her home now, for as long as she wants it."

"Good. I'll see you Friday evening, then."

"In time for dinner?" asked Annabelle.

"Of course. You don't think I'm giving up the chance of trying your cooking again, do you?" Lars gave her a mischievous grin, and Annabelle glowed with pride.

"All right, be off with you," said Niels gruffly. "I'm sure Karen will see you out."

Together they moved to the front door and

down the path to the gate. Lars paused a moment, looking down at Karen, and she held her breath. Oh, dear, she thought, is he going to kiss me? And if he does, should I merely accept it graciously, or respond with the warmth that I feel for him? Because I do feel something very strong for him...

"Karen, this has been a wonderful day for me." He put his hand on her arm. "It's been great meeting you. And your uncle again, too. And Annabelle..." His voice trailed off and he stared down at her face, glowing faintly in the moonlight. Karen looked up at him, and with a single movement, they moved closer until her lips met, blended and lingered for a breathless moment; then he pulled away.

"I'll see you Friday afternoon, late," he whispered. "Take care now."

"You, too. Drive safely."

He climbed in the car and drove away slowly with a wave of his hand. Karen stood, staring after the taillights until they were out of sight; then she turned and walked slowly back into the house.

Annabelle noticed the expression on her face and grinned. "Well, well," she commented loudly. "I presume that young man has left his mark upon you."

"Oh, be quiet, Annabelle." Niels glared at her in mock annoyance. "I'm sure Karen's old enough to know what she's doing."

"No woman's ever old enough for that," Annabelle retorted equably. "And he is very handsome. You sure know how to pick 'em, my dear."

Karen flushed and sat down at the table while Annabelle bustled around with the coffee cups. "I didn't pick him," she said calmly. "I think he picked me."

"Oh-oh." Niels raised his eyebrows humorously. "A pickup, eh? You'd better watch yourself, my girl."

"He is very nice," Karen admitted. "And I do like him a lot already. Which sounds ridiculous, I suppose," she added apologetically. "We only met today. Yet somehow, I feel like I've known him all my life."

Niels nodded. "I know the feeling. That's how it was with Annabelle and me. When she moved to Uppsala two years ago, we bumped into each other in the cafeteria one day. I mean that literally, by the way. We both were carrying our trays to a table, neither of us looking where we were going, and the next thing, she had bean soup all over her dress and I had ruined a pair of my finest white trousers with spaghetti." He chuckled. "A disastrous first meeting. She barely contained herself, and knowing her as I do now, I'm surprised she didn't let fly and cuss me out soundly."

"I was so nervous, I couldn't speak," said Annabelle, bringing the coffee to the table and pouring three cups of the tantalizing, steaming brew. "I had only been on the faculty about a week. I hardly knew anyone, and was trying desperately to maintain my dignity. You know how it is with a new teacher. You have to create a good impression at first. After they know you, you can raise all kinds of hell and get away with murder if you want to. But then..." She giggled. "I was trying to behave like the prim English matron I'm supposed to me. And this character bangs into me like that. Well, let me tell you..." She shrugged. "Anyway, we sat down together and by the time we'd finished our lunch, I think we knew exactly how we felt towards each other. The next night I cooked his dinner for him, and I haven't stopped since."

Niels leaned over and squeezed her arm affectionately. "You're quite a woman, you know that?"

"I do," she replied inperturbably, giving Karen a broad wink.

"You see..." Niels sighed and gave Karen a despairing look. "Once you let them in the front door, you can't get rid of them. Take heed, Karen, with that young man of yours. He had a look in his eye."

"I should hope so," Annabelle broke in loudly. "She's only the most beautiful girl who's set foot in Uppsala in years. And Lars is going to have some competition, if you ask me. Once Karen sets foot on the campus, she'll have them banging on the front door morning, noon and night."

"Which reminds me," Niels said, carefully sipping his coffee. "You are planning to start school here, right?"

Karen nodded. "Just as soon as I can," she replied.

"Well, that may present a problem. We've just started our summer semester, and the classes are all full. That I do know. It might be wise if you waited til the fall. That will give you the advantage of settling down for a couple of months, which, I believe, might be the best thing in the long run."

Karen frowned. "I'm sorry to hear that. I was really looking forward to starting school right away."

"Look. You've just arrived. It's going to take

you weeks to adjust to the change. Living in Sweden is a lot different to the United States, believe me. I presume you don't speak the language?" Niels looked at her enquiringly. Karen shook her head.

"I used to know a little, back when I was a child. Mother and dad used to speak it now and then. But..." She shrugged. "I don't even remember a single expression any longer."

"I thought so. So why not take a course in Swedish this summer—that you can get easily enough—and prepare yourself for entering classes in the fall? I mean, there are classes that are taught in English, but for getting around, talking to people, you should be able to speak Swedish. It's not difficult. I'm sure you'll pick it up in no time."

Karen thought a moment. "Maybe you're right," she murmured, tasting her coffee, which was delicious.

"I've got another idea," said Annabelle. "Why not get yourself a job? It will keep you busy, and also help you with the language, and give you an idea of the people. Maybe some job involving the public, perhaps."

Niels shook hishead. "I don't think Karen needs that," he began, but Karen interrupted him. "Wait, Uncle Niels. Annabelle may have something there. It would certainly be a good way to get to know the people, you must agree. I think that's worth considering."

He shook his head adamantly. "I don't think so, Karen. You have plenty of money. What do you have to go to work for?"

"For the reason we've just been talking about, you ninny," said Annabelle explosively. "It'll help her adjust, and after what she has been through, I think she needs something like that. You're gone all day at school. So am I. What's she going to do with herself, for heaven's sake?"

"It sounds like I'm overruled." Niels gave Karen a glum smile. "Anyway, there's lots of time to decide." He glanced at his watch. "Talking of time, you must be getting sleepy. All that travel today, and the jetlag and everything."

"Frankly, I am ready for bed," Karen admitted. "If you two won't think me rude, I think I'd like to turn in."

Niels waved her way carelessly. "Go ahead. In this house, you do what you want. Everyone does," he added with a meaningful glance at Annabelle. "Give your uncle a kiss."

Karen bent down and hugged him. "Goodnight," she said, "and thank you, too, Annabelle. The dinner was out of sight."

"See you in the morning, then."

Karen made her way to the bedroom, undressed and, silencing her conscience, decided to forego any bathroom activities; that could wait till the morning. With a sigh of infinite relief, she slid between the sheets. It had been a tumultuous twenty-four hours since she left Chicago. The trip to London. Meeting Lars. The flight to Stockholm. The drive to Uppsala. Seeing Uncle Niels again, and meeting Annabelle.

It had all been so wonderful, she thought sleepily. Especially meeting Lars. What a handsome man he was, and how thrilling it had been, that brief kiss at the gate before he left. She wondered how soon it would be before she could kiss him again...

With his face smiling at her in her mind, she slid into a deep sleep.

CHAPTER 5

Karen awoke and blinked her eyes vaguely, staring around and feeling, for a few seconds, disoriented, not knowing where she was, what day it was...then everything fell into place and she sat up in the bed, stretching her arms happily. She had slept like a log, as her father used to say—a deep, dreamless sleep that had restored her energies and her spirits. She slipped out of bed, rummaged in her suitcase for her robe and after a quick visit to the bathroom, she padded down the hallway in her slippers and into the kitchen. The clock on the wall pointed to eight-fifteen, and there was a pot of steaming coffee on the stove. The kitchen door was open, and she went outside, breathing the crisp, pure air with delight. At the far end of the property she saw a small, red-painted barn, and next to it was the stocky figure of her uncle, carrying a sack of feed inside.

"Hi, Uncle Niels!" she called out, waving. He paused, looked back towards the house, and waved. "Be with you in a little while," he shouted. She nodded, went back inside and poured herself some coffee, sitting at the table and gathering her thoughts. She felt particularly cheerful, and smiled to herself contentedly as she looked around the room, admiring the picturesque touches that, she felt sure, were Annabelle's doing. The gay chintz curtains over the windows; the little shelf a couple of feet from the ceiling, on which some obviously local carvings stood, adding a festive touch to the decor. She went over and lifted a statue down: a brightly painted wooden carving of a mountain climber, complete to the last detail of hose, leather jacket and a miniature alpenstock in his hands. The statue reminded Karen of the intricate Bavarian carvings her parents had brought back after their tour of Austria a few years ago. Such delicacy, she thought, and she pictured the craftsman, sitting bent over his workbench, carving tool in hand, patiently producing this minor work of art. Why was it the Europeans kept the old skills alive, oblivious to the heartless march of progress that had wiped out so many handicrafts in America? Perhaps that was the basic difference between the countries—America forging ahead with mass-produced items designed for the dime store markets, while in Europe, men still preserved their artistic heritage, working with their hands, uninhibited by economic considerations... It was an interesting thought.

"Well, you're up." Karen smiled at her uncle as he walked into the kitchen and went over to the sink to wash his hands. "Sleep well?"

Karen nodded. "Oh, yes. I didn't realize how tired I was."

Niels nodded. "Those transatlantic flights can be exhausting. It's odd, they've got the Concorde now—what's it? Three hours from New York to London then passengers spend eight hours in bed, catching up. It all seems such a ridiculous exercise in convenience." He grinned. "But then, that's progress, as they say."

Karen laughed quietly. "I was thinking that very thing when you walked in. These carvings..." She rose, replacing the statue on the shelf above her head. "They're absolutely beautiful, and I was wondering why we don't have things like this in the States."

Niels grinned and wiped his hands on a towel.

"I'm glad you don't," he remarked. "It would kill all the tourist sales each year. Why do you think Americans come to Europe every year? They go back loaded with all these quaint little items we make here." His face grew serious. "That's part of the difference in the cultures, as you will find out. In fact, it could be an interesting subject for your thesis one day, provided you get your doctorate, of course. But the difference between caring about how something is made and the slapdash methods of mass production have always intrigued me. Certainly there is more quality in European manufacture. Perhaps we take more time, but then, we wind up with a product that we're proud of. Something that will last. Look at that car your friend was drving yesterday—the Volvo. They are built to last ten, twelve years—and they do. Show me any American car that doesn't fall apart after five years." He laughed cynically. "What do they call it? Built-in obsolescence, eh? I'm afraid I don't agree with that very much."

He hung the towel back on the rail, straightened it neatly and turned to face Karen. "Well, my dear, can I fix you some breakfast?"

"That would be nice, but let me do it. I'm a good cook, really."

"If you'd prefer. We have everything here in the refrigerator. And I'm sure you know how to operate the electric stove."

Karen nodded. "If I don't, I'll ask," she replied gaily. "What about you? Can I fix some eggs and bacon for you, too?"

"Yes, that would be great. I usually eat at the cafeteria in the university, but I'd much prefer eating here with you." He looked at her with a warmth in his eyes that made Karen glow. "It's going to be wonderful having you around, Karen." He gave her a quick hug. "You know, I always envied your father, having such a beautiful daughter. I know I can never step into his shoes, but I'm going to try, let me tell you."

"How come you never married, Uncle Niels?" Karen asked curiously, going to the refrigerator and taking out a package of bacon.

He shrugged. "Too wrapped up in my work, I suppose. I'm one of these dedicated professor types, you know... There was a girl in college, but..." He pursed his lips and paused a moment, letting a nostalgic expression creep over his face. "Well, that was a long time ago. Too long ago to start regretting at this point in tme. Besides, I have Annabelle now, and she's about the best thing that's come into my life in years. Quite an extraordinary woman, I must say. I hope you two become good friends."

"I'm sure we will," said Karen. "I like her very much already."

She took a skillet from the cabinet and put it on the stove with the bacon. "I've been thinking," Karen continued after turning on the heat under the pan. "About school, and what Annabelle said last night. You know, about getting a job."

"I don't think it's such a good idea," said Niels.

"I do. I can't sit around here all day."

"You can take my car and explore the area. You've got enough to keep you busy for weeks."

Karen wrinkled her nose. "That'd get old very quickly," she said firmly. "I don't see wandering around by myself. Besides, Lars said he would take me out on weekends and show me around."

"Hm..." Niels looked at her speculatively. "You're quite keen on this young man, I take it?"

"I like him, yes. nothing serious, though."

"I should hope not," Niels grunted. "Although he does seem a good type. But you can never tell these days..."

"I'm going to find out all I can about him," Karen continued, turning the bacon, "but I do believe he's a good person. We had a long talk yesterday. We have a lot in common, really. It rather surprised me."

"Yes," Niels said with a skeptical tone in his voice, "but then he may surprise you in another way. Forgive me for sounding cynical, my dear, but you are a most attractive young woman. Lars would have to be a little strange if he weren't interested in you. And that interest has nothing to do with your intellectual capacities. You've probably heard about the liberal attitudes young people have in Sweden towards relationships?"

Karen nodded. "I know about that, Uncle Neils. But don't worry. I'm not going to move in with Lars. I may take an apartment of my own," she added, "but then, that's something in the future."

Niels looked at her sadly. "You...you're not thinking of getting a place right away, surely?" he asked. "I mean, you can stay here as long as you like, Karen. I want you to regard this as your home now, beleive me."

"I know, and I appreciate that very much." Karen began removing the bacon from the pan and placing it on two plates. "But I'm not planning to move in for good. You know that, surely? I mean, you have your life and I have mine. I'll be getting a place eventually."

Niels shook his head. "You're a Christensen, all right," he murmured. "Independent, stubborn." His face broke into a smile. "And I understand.

Annabelle and I talked about this many times these past few weeks. She knows I would just as soon you moved in for good, but she was quick to point out that there could be certain problems. I am, let's face it, rather set in my ways. I think Annabelle's the only woman who could stand me for any length of time. She's learned to adapt, as it were, but then, she's close to my own age. You're so much younger. You're going to have a lot of young friends, especially when you start school again. It would only restrict your social life if you were living here, much as I would love to have you around."

"I know. But you have Annabelle." Karen reached for the eggs and began breaking them into the pan. "How d'you like your eggs, by the way?"

"Anyway, as long as they're not runny." Niels rose and moved to the cabinet, taking out the bread. "I'll make the toast." He took a knife and expertly sliced four pieces off the large loaf, placing them in the electric toaster-oven on the counter. He stood back, observing Karen as she turned the eggs in the pan. He smiled.

"You handle those extremely well," he said. "Maybe you should get a job as a cook."

Karen laughed. "No, thanks. I enjoy cooking, but I'd hate it if I had to stand behind a counter eight hours and cook a hundred hamburgers. No, Uncle Niels, I'd like some job where I meet people, be able to talk with them and learn something about the customs over here."

"You sound very determined. You've made up your mind, then, I gather?"

"I think so. I'm not going to start looking for a few days, though. But after a week or so, I'm sure something will turn up. Maybe you or Annabelle will hear of a suitable position."

"Possibly."

She served the eggs on the plates and carried them to the table. Niels took the toast from the oven, buttered it quickly and brought it to the table. He sat down, his eyes sparkling. "This does look good," he observed with pleasure. "Our first breakfast together, Karen. I hope there'll be many more."

"Of course there will, Uncle Niels."

They finished their breakfast and Niels excused himself, dressing quickly and leaving for his first class at the university. "I'll be back around noon," he promised. "Just make yourself at home and relax."

Karen watched him drive away in his smart little Saab station wagon; then she closed the front door and went back to her bedroom. She unpacked her clothes, took a shower and returned to the kitchen to wash up the breakfast dishes. She was feeling thoroughly at home already, and looked around with a glow of happiness at the cosy atmosphere of the house. It was definitely a man's house, she realized, but with little touches of color and style that obviously were Annabelle's doing. Which reminded her: she felt sure Uncle Niels would have left his bed unmade, just as her father used to do.

She made her way down the hallway into her uncle's room at the end and stared, aghast, at the rumpled bedclothes; the oddments of clothing and underwear scattered around; the general air of untidiness. "Well," she said aloud. "We can't have this, can we?"

She set to work, straightening the bed, folding the trousers and hanging them in the closet, and carrying the underwear to the hamper in the bathroom. It didn't take long, and she finally stood back by the door, admiring her handiwork. The room was tidy and looked more like she felt the bedroom of a respected professor *should* look...but then she realized by the following morning, it would probably revert to its original condition. As Uncle Niels had said, he was set in his ways... At least it was an effort to repay him for his kindness and hospitality, she felt. The least she could do while she stayed here, was to clean up the place each day. In any case, she rather enjoyed housework. She hoped Annabelle did, too, because if she did marry Uncle Niels, she would have her hands full keeping the place in shape after moving in...

She looked at her wrist watch and saw that it was 11:30. Uncle Niels would probably be home soon. She was unsure whether or not he had afternoon classes, but in any case, she felt he would appreciate having lunch ready when he returned. She made her way to the kitchen, opened the refrigerator and inspected the contents. There was a variety of cheeses, some cold meats and jars of salad dressing and mayonnaise. Plus plenty of lettuce, tomatoes and carrots. Plenty for sandwiches, she realized, and she set to work, slicing the bread and getting the meal ready. She grinned to herself, remembering the sliced bread back in the States; it was a convenience, she thought, but then, was it such a chore to slice bread? A small item, perhaps, but it could well be the first of many differences she would undoubtedly encounter as she adapted to her new land.

She finished making the sandwiches, and as an

afterthought, she made a small salad, tossing it in the large cut-glass bowl she found in the cabinet. She set two places at the table, put the salad in the middle and stood back, admiring the effect. At that moment, she heard a car pull up in front and seconds later, Uncle Niels bounced into the house, dumping an armful of books in a chair and coming into the kitchen, breathing heavily. He saw the table and grinned.

"Well, isn't this nice?" he said, giving Karen a quick kiss on the cheek. "A regular little housekeeper, aren't you?" He chuckled. You'll make some lucky man a good wife one of these days, I can see."

Without any ceremony, he sat down and began chomping on a sandwich, nodding his head with enthusiastic approval. Karen made the coffee and brought it over, and sat down herself, her eyes shining happily at his obvious delight.

"Do you have to go back to the university this afternoon?" she asked.

Niels shook his head. "No. I'm done for the day," he replied. "I thought this afternoon I might take you around and show you a little of Uppsala."

"That would be wonderful, thank you."

They finished their lunch, and Karen cleared away the dishes. Niels lit his pipe and relaxed, watching her fondly as she washed the plates and put them in the drainer. "I expect you miss a dishwasher," he observed with a chuckle.

"Not really," Karen replied.

"There are a lot of American appliances you'll find we manage without," he told her. "And as far as a dishwasher is concerned, I think they're great for large families. But with just me..." He shrugged. "It would take me a week to fill it up."

"Don't worry. I don't mind it a bit. In fact, I've had a lot of fun this morning, cleaning house."

Niels frowned. "Now, Karen, you haven't..." He stood up quickly, and disappeared into the livingroom. Karen heard him stomping down the hall and into his bedroom. Moments later, he returned, a grateful grin on his face. "I don't know what to say, except thanks," he said. "That's the first time my bedroom's been cleaned in ages. I do have a woman who comes in once a week, but she's been ill for over a month."

"I'm surprised you haven't got Annabelle to take over," said Karen. "She looks like she'd do anything for you."

"True. But her adoration stops short of cleaning house," Niels replied. "Annabelle's a magnificent cook, a wonderful companion but she's hopeless at housework. I know if we ever get married, I'll still have to employ a domestic. You see, Annabelle's working on a book. She's quite brilliant, really, despite that rather frothy exterior. A deep thinker, and an outstanding instructor. She's very well respected by the faculty."

"I'm surprised she isn't married."

"Oh, she was, years ago. Her husband died, though. He was a contractor or builder or something in Ipswich. Annabelle went back to school, got her degrees and began teaching. She's often said she wished she'd done it years before. She loves teaching."

"You'll make a good couple," said Karen mischievously.

"Now, listen here, young lady." Niels glared at her with mock disapproval. "No more of this marriage talk, you hear? Annabelle and I will make it legal in our own good time. Until then, we happen to enjoy a remarkably cordial relationship. And if you start hinting all the time, she's liable to think I put you up to it. So please, Karen, leave well enough alone."

"I was only kidding."

"I know. But Annabelle is English, and they don't always understand the American sense of humor. Surely you know this from your studies of differing cultures? What makes Americans laugh often leaves the English staring blankly, wondering what was so funny..." He smiled at Karen. "And, as you will discover, the Swedes have their peculiarities, too. Anyway, as far as Annabelle is concerned, stay away from cute remarks about marrige."

Karen frowned. "I understand, Uncle Niels. But you're making quite an issue of it. I got the impression Annabelle was a rather broad-minded, jolly sort of woman."

"She is. Outrageously so, at times. But when it comes to the subject of our relationship, she can be curiously withdrawn. To be honest, Karen," Niels said, his voice softening slightly, "she's in love with me. She's wanted us to get married for months, but..." His voice trailed off. "I just haven't felt it would be a good idea at the moment."

"Don't you love her?"

"Yes, I do. Very much, in fact. But being the crusty old bachelor that I am. I have to ease myself into it gradually. Which is why Annabelle's been here so often. She's done some decorating in the house, which amuses her, so I don't object. In fact. I rather enjoy what she's done to the house. I believe when we know all we should about each other, and decide we can stand each other on a permanent basis, then perhaps she can move in." He paused, and an awkward expression crossed his face. "You see, Karen, at your age, marriage isn't such an adjustment. Two young people can grow and adapt to each other far easier than two older people, who are used to a certain pattern of existence."

"Does Annabelle share this attitude of yours?"

"Not completely. You see, she was married before. And women are, in reality, far more adaptable than men. No, Karen, I'm the stick-in-the-mud. If Annabelle had her way, we'd have been married a long time ago. But I have to be sure I don't spoil her life, and at the same time, complicate my own beyond endurance."

"You sound as though you enjoy living alone?"

"I do. I have my work, my reading, my little farm here. I am, really, quite content. As for having someone to scratch my back at night, well..." He gave her a mischievous glance. "I had my share of that when I was a young man. I've never thought of getting married merely to satisfy those urges which, quite frankly, have waned somewhat over the past few years." He chuckled. "That may sound very odd to you. To any young person, for that matter."

Karen shook her head. "No, I think I understand. I remember daddy saying once that if two people can't get along outside the bedroom, sex isn't going to make much difference to their relationship."

"Your father was a wise man. And obviously he brought you up with the right ideas. He must have been very proud of you, Karen, just as I am. You're a fine young woman."

Karen blushed. "Thank you, Uncle Niels."

"Anyway, enough philosophizing for one afternoon," he said, pushing his chair back and standing up quickly. "Come on, I want to show you around the town. I think you'll enjoy seeing it. Especially the university. It's one of the prettiest campuses I know."He paused a moment. "Oh, while I think of it," he added. "Your young man. Lars, is that his name?"

Karen nodded. "Lars Tengborn. He's not really my young man, Uncle Niels. We just met."

"Maybe so, but I get the feeling you're quite taken with him. And he, obviously, is going to pursue the friendship. I thought you'd like to know I think he's a very appealing person, but don't get too involved. You've got your schooling to complete. I don't mean to interfere, but I've been thinking about this all morning. I just don't want you to get carried away. You have too much ahead of you."

Karen nodded. "Don't worry, Uncle Niels. Like yourself, I plan to stay single for quite a while."

"Good. Now let's get going."

He closed up the house, locked the front door and within five minutes, they were whizzing down the street towards the campus. Karen felt the crisp air blowing through her hair, and she breathed deeply, feeling a rich glow of contentment permeate her body. This was her first day in Uppsala; her first day in Sweden, and already she felt so at home, like she had lived here all her life. Was it because, as her father had told her once, we are only truly happy and feel we belong on the soil that nurtured our family roots?

She listened attentively as Uncle Niels began describing the various buildings they passed, pointing out the different departments at the university. Later, as they drove around the town, he showed her the many historical landmarks dating back to an earlier erea. Interested as she was, she found her mind wandering, her thoughts straying to Stockholm and to Lars. What was he doing at this moment? Was he thinking of her, just as she was picturing him? She had told Uncle Niels she did not intend getting serious with Lars. Yet here he was, monopolizing her thoughts and sparking a delicious anticipation of the coming weekend. Karen knew the days would not pass quickly enough for her. She longed to see him again. Foolish as she knew it was, she couldn't help it... Maybe, despite her rationalizing, she had fallen in love with him...

CHAPTER 6

By the time Friday night arrived, Karen had settled down very comfortably to the routine of her uncle's home. Annabelle came in every evening to prepare the meal, something she insisted on doing by herself while Niels and Karen sipped sherry in the livingroom and chatted. Karen was allowed to help with the washing up afterwards, however, a chore that Annabelle frankly admitted bored her to distraction. "I just love fixing all those precious little goodies for the table," she said, "but to wash dishes? Ugh!" She shuddered. "It makes me think I'm a scullery maid, and that's the last thing I see myself becoming. Not for any man," she added, with a coy glance at Niels, who pretended to ignore her remarks and continued puffing his pipe imperturbably.

They really had an ideal relationship, Karen decided after the first two days. Apart from actually sharing a bedroom, they might as well be man and wife: they saw each other every day, both at home and at the university; they exchanged occasional loving glances when they thought Karen wasn't watching; their arguements were little more than surface bickering caused mostly by Annabelle's acerbic tongue and Niels' stuffiness, pretended or real; in all, they reminded Karen of her own parents, and the similarity was all the more affecting because of her uncle's close resemblance to her father.

Karen cleaned house every morning, after which she would either relax in the enormous garden, puttering among the flowers, or taking long walks around the neighborhood. She found herself blending into the lifestyle very quickly, absorbing the little nuances of behavior and attitudes from Niels and from Annabelle, whose chief concern seemed to be that their new arrival enjoy herself to the fullest; but they needn't have worried. Karen admitted that she had never felt happier in her life. While she would naturally hold dear the many memories of her life in Minneapolis with her parents, she could not recall ever feeling so completely at ease, with such a sense of belonging. And it was more than Niels' daily efforts to please her; it was, she felt, a spiritual awareness that she was in the right place in the world, among her right kind of people.

She accompanied Annabelle to the stores, and found that many of the sales clerks spoke English, and were only too happy to converse with her. While Uppsala was not a large city, there was a distinctly international flavor to it, blending with the traditional Swedish ambiance that permeated every area of life. Uppsala University was the oldest in Scandinavia, renowned as a scientific center and as a result, it had attracted men and women from all parts of the world, both students as well as instructors. They helped add a cosmopolitan atmosphere, imparting a vibrancy and excitement that provided an intriguing contrast to the staid and traidtional flavor of the city.

"You certainly seem to have fallen in love with our little corner of the world," Niels said to Karen one evening after she had spoken at length on her reactions since her arrival—comments which, she knew, pleased her uncle immeasurably.

"I have," she admitted. "It's everything I ever dreamed it might be. A perfect place to live, really."

Annabelle snorted. "Wait until winter comes, duckie," she said. "You'll change your mind fast. It's not going to be much fun trudging to school with snow up to your bottom."

"It's not quite that bad," Niels said placatingly. "But we do have a lot of snow."

"So what?" Karen retorted. "We get snow in Minnesota. Last winter was especially bad. Many towns were practically closed down for days. In any case, I enjoy winter sports, and I plan to do a lot of skiing. Lars told me he knows some good slopes around here."

Annabelle raised an eyebrow and looked at Niels. "No matter what we talk about," she said caustically, but with a twinkle in her eyes. "She always manages to bring that young man into the conversation. I'll be so glad when Friday gets here and he'll take her off our hands."

"So will I," said Karen fervently. "I'm so anxious to see Stockholm. In fact, I hope Lars takes me in and shows me the sights."

"Oh, you mean you're going to Stockholm for the weekend?" Niels looked at her questioningly.

"I don't know what we'll be doing," Karen replied truthfully, "but I hope we do go there. I never even got a glimpse of it from the air. And Lars has told me some wonderful things about the city."

"It is impressive," Niels said. "A city of contrasts, really. Tall, sterile modern buildings side-by-side with poky old Swedish houses, hotels and mansions that have been turned into apartments. Very picturesque. I think you'll enjoy it." He hesitated a moment. "When is Lars coming?"

"Friday night, I suppose," said Karen. "Or late afternoon. He didn't say, really."

"And if you go to Stockholm, I presume you'll come back here afterwards?"

Annabelle shushed him with a flip of her hand. "Now, Niels, I know what you're leading up to, and it's none of your business. If Karen stays overnight, she can certainly take care of herself."

Karen nodded. "Don't worry, Uncle Niels," she murmured. "I'm not planning a weekend of sin with Lars. He's just going to show me around, that's all."

Niels cleared his throat awkwardly. "I didn't mean to pry, my dear, but you don't know much about this young man..."

"Which is why," Annabelle interrupted him loudly, "she is going out with him. And when she does find out more about him, let her make up her own mind whether she wants to do anything more than hold hands. He's such an old-fashioned fuddy-duddy, my dear," she added, turning to Karen with a conspiratorial smirk.

That Friday, Karen awoke with a pulse-pounding expectancy in her heart. She packed Uncle Niels off to school, and at once began cleaning and dusting, going through the entire house from front door to back porch, making sure that everything was spotless, shiny and smelling clean and fresh. She giggled to herself: a proper little housewife, she thought, trying to create the best impression for a visitor. Only this wasn't just a visitor. This was Lars, and by now, she knew beyond any doubt that he was someone very special to her.

She chuckled over Uncle Niels' concerns about the weekend. He was worse than her father had been! Fancy his suspecting she intended going off to a hotel with Lars and only taking one room! Upon reflection, she concluded that his attitude was possibly sparked by the liberal attitudes in Sweden among the young people—and that his prim admonitions were merely the understandable emotional backlash from someone of an older generation, not quite approving of the present changes in the moral climate.

But whatever the youth of Sweden, Denmark and Norway might consider acceptable behavior between unmarried couples, Karen did not intend to discard her long-standing principles of propriety. And despite the impulsive kiss between her and Lars, she felt he was not the type of man to take advantage of a girl. Certainly he wouldn't turn down an available bed partner when the occasion arose—after all, there was no hint of lasciviousness in his nature, but still, he was, she felt, a normal male with normal urges—but the idea of him forcing his attentions upon her was unthinkable. He was, she suspected, what her mother would have termed "a nice young man", meaning someone who had been blessed with proper parental guidance in his youth and who regarded a woman's virtue as inviolable until after marriage. Which, as far as Karen was concerned, was the best way to be, the only way she could be...

She gave a final approving glance at the small guest room behind the kitchen. She had put clean linen on the bed, straightened the covers and plumped the pillows and put fresh towels on the night stand. The final touch: a small vase of fresh flowers on the chest of drawers—daisies and maidenhair fern which she had found in a secluded corner of the back garden.

She glanced at her wrist watch, amazed that it was 11:30 already. The morning had simply flown! She hurried to the kitchen to begin preparing lunch for Uncle Niels. She had no idea when Lars would arrive, but she presumed it would be late afternoon or early evening. He probably left work at five, and considering the weekend traffic on the highway, he might only arrive in Uppsala at 6:30, possibly later. She anticipated their spending the evening with Uncle Niels and Annabelle, and going back to Stockholm in the morning. Whether they would stay overnight on Saturday and return Sunday would depend on whatever Lars had planned for them. It was useless to speculate. She would just have to await his arrival, and she hoped the afternoon would slip by as quickly as the morning. Oh, but she was longing to see him again...

Before Uncle Niels returned to the university after lunch for a faculty meeting, he remarked on the appearance of the house. "If nothing else, you can stay here and work for me," he said, grinning, his eyes roaming around the livingroom with obvious appreciation. "Or don't you fancy working as a domestic?"

"Get out of here," Karen said pleasantly, giving him a quick kiss on the cheek and pushing him towards the front door. But she felt a glow of satisfaction that her work had been noticed.

She washed up the lunch dishes, put them away and went back to her room. She decided to take a nap as they would undoubtedly be up late that night, talking. She lay down and within minutes, had fallen asleep. She awoke at four-thirty to the sound of Annabelle rattling around in the kitchen. Sleepily, Karen went in and put the water on for a cup of tea. Annabelle greeted her warmly.

"All set for your visitor?" she said, her eyes twinkling merrily. "It looks as though six maids went through this house. Are you by any chance hinting that I don't keep the place clean?"

"Oh, Annabelle..." Karen looked at the older woman with mild disapproval. "I just did a little dusting and polishing."

"Getting the palace in order for Prince Charming, eh?" Annabelle gave a raucous laugh. "Oh, my, the pangs of young love..." She shook her head. "Let me clue you, young lady. You could be living in a stable. It makes no difference. It's you he's coming to see."

"I know. But I like everything to be just so."

"All right, I understand. I'm only pulling your leg."

They sat down at the kitchen table and had a cup of tea together; then Annabelle began busying herself with preparing dinner.

"I'll have enough for Lars if he arrives before we eat," she told Karen. "But I don't expect him until later, really. On Friday afternoons, the highway is crowded to capacity with cars getting out of Stockholm for the weekend. Don't look for him before eight or nine." She saw the look of frustration appear fleetingly on Karen's face. "On the other hand, my dear, he may just surprise us and come barrelling in here in the next fifteen minutes." She chuckled. "I know how you feel, my dear. I was the same when I was going with my late husband—before we married, that is." She got out the roast from the refrigerator and began readying it for the oven. "Oh, you should have seen me. I was only seventeen, and very impressionable. I'd be all of a hoo-hah every afternoon until he came to the house and took me to the cinema, or to the library, or wherever he decided would be a good place for us to be alone. Sometimes we'd go into the woods. Those were the best times." A far-off look entered her eyes and she looked sad for a moment, Karen noticed. "He was such a good man, really. Earthy and impulsive, which I appreciated at that age, but later, when we both grew up, I realized he was everything any woman could have wished for in a husband. But the courting days were the best. They always are. That sort of love is only for the young. The sort of insane, light-headed feeling that chases your reason and makes you think of nothing else. Right?"

Karen nodded. "Right. It's rather stupid, really. Or I feel it is, because I've never reacted like this before, not to any man."

Annabelle glanced at her curiously. "Don't tell me you've never been in love before?"

"Not like this. There was a boy in high school. His name was Kevin and he was the star athlete. Tall, muscular, handsome..."

"Stop it, my dear, you're getting me dithery."

Karen laughed at Annabelle's pretended confusion. "Anyway, it turned out he was only after the inevitable. I thought he liked me and instead all he wanted was..."

"I know. I've had my share of those." Annabelle sniffed contemptuously. "I won't deny we all share our basic urges, but if we gave in to them the way some boys do, imagine what a mess the world would be in. And in my case, I believe a man respects a girl far more in the long run, if she doesn't flip her skirts for him every time they get together. It's like any pleasure in life, my dear. Anticipation is more than half the fun." She glanced shrewdly at Karen. "As far as Lars is concerned, I am really quite surprised you feel so strongly about him. In these last few days, I've got the impression you're a very sensible young woman."

"I am. Which is why this feeling is so frustrating," said Karen.

"Oh, well, there has to be a first time for everyone," said Annabelle philosophically. "At least he has my approval. If I were twenty years younger, I'd have a go at him myself. I've always liked blondes," she added with a giggle.

"He is so nice," Karen agreed. "And I was very surprised at his age. I thought he was only a few years older than me. He's actually twenty-nine, he told me."

"That so? Well, well, he doesn't look it. But then, that's all to the good. I've always felt it best for a husband to be at least five years older than his wife, if not more. That gives him a chance to get some sense into his head. Between you and me, Karen, I've always felt women are smarter than men. We have more resiliency, more ability to handle adversity and we also live longer."

Karen laughed. "Spoken like a true Women's Libber."

Annabelle's eyes flashed. "Nonsense! I may be liberal, but I'm no women's libber. Marching around with signs and wearing blue jeans and scruffy clothes? Not me, never. I'll agree women deserve equal pay for equal work, but there are some jobs meant for men, some for women. Nothing wrong with a natural division of labor like that, don't you think?" She lifted the pan with the roast—a delicious leg of lamb surrounded by peeled potatoes and carrots—and popped it in the oven with a satisfied sigh. "There, that should be ready abut seven, I'd say." She smiled at Karen. "So if your Lothario comes riding up on his white horse by then, he can eat with us."

"I hope he does." Karen looked up as the noise of a car engine broke the stillness outside the house. "Maybe that's him now."

Annabelle shook her head. "That's the Saab engine. They make that funny little put-put sound. So relax. It's only Niels."

A few minutes later, Niels clomped into the livingroom, mumbling under his breath. He came through to the kitchen. "Tea?" he said loudly. "Just what I need." He collapsed into a chair and Karen got a cup and saucer and poured for him. Annabelle looked at him curiously. "Something wrong, Niels?" she asked.

"Oh, nothing, really. Just those idiotic faculty members. They're like a bunch of old women."

Annabelle bristled. "And what's wrong with old women?" she demanded, turning to Karen. "You see? What were we just talking about?"

"You know what I mean, Annabelle," he sighed. "I try to get something worked out for my department, and they behave like I'm asking for the moon." He took a sip from his tea and nodded. "Good. This'll restore my spirits." He managed to smile at Karen. "And what have you two been up to all afternoon?"

"I've been sleeping," said Karen. "Annabelle's fixed dinner. Roast lamb. Your favorite."

Niels reached out and squeezed Annabelle's arm as she passed the table. "She knows what I like, don't you?"

"I should hope so," she retorted, stifling the grin that threatened to spread over her face. "There's very little I don't know about you, Niels Christensen." Their eyes met and Karen wondered whether she would one day be exchanging a glance of such obvious affection with some man—maybe Lars, maybe someone she had yet to meet. She felt warm and tender inside at the knowledge of her uncle's good fortune in having a woman like Annabelle. This was part of the overall happiness she felt was part of this house, part of the joy she shared merely by being here.

"Well, I'm going to clean up a little and change my dress," Karen said, rising and moving towards the hallway.

"Yes, you do that, dear," said Annabelle. "Your best ball gown, no doubt." She winked at Niels. "You wouldn't believe what a dither this girl's been in all day."

Karen went to her room and sat on the bed a moment, debating what she would wear. Why am I like this? she wondered, annoyed with herself for turning into a simpering idiot at the thought that very soon now, Lars would arrive. She took hold of herself, went to the closet and finally selected a light blue shirt-waist dress that matched her eyes, and a pair of gold leather low heels, almost the same color as her hair. She checked her makeup, added a little shadow to her eyelids and felt she was, at last, ready to receive Lars. She had a feeling he would not be late arriving, and she was right. Annabelle had just taken the lamb out of the oven, and was busily making the gravy when there was a knock at the door. Karen rushed to open it and there, on the front step, stood Lars. Her first impulse was to move forward into his arms. Instead she stood, staring at the soft smile of happiness on his lips, her eyes sparkling with joy. "Come in, come in," she urged him, "you're just in time for dinner."

He walked past her into the livingroom, and she let her glance refresh her memory of his broad shoulders and lean, tapered body that moved easily and with such masculine grace.

Niels rose and shook hands. "Good to see you again, Lars," he said. "Sherry?"

"Please." Lars dropped nonchalantly into a chair and lit a cigarette. Karen sat down nervously on the couch, staring at him, and wondering why he had seemed so casual when he arrived; why he had not said a single word to her. Not that she needed it, seeing the look in his eyes; but she did want him to say something...

"Good to see you again, Karen," he murmured at last. He took a sip from his sherry, set it down and leaned back with a sigh.

"Tired?" asked Niels, staring at Lars curiously.

Lars nodded. "Very much so, I'm afraid," he responded. "I've had a rather exhausting week. I almost called to put off our visit," he added, looking at Karen.

"Oh. I'm sorry," she said, feeling suddenly rather deflated. "If you'd rather..."

"No, no. I'm here now. I'll probably perk up after some of Annabelle's cooking." He managed a weak smile as Annabelle popped her head around the door and winked at him. "Be ready in a few minutes," she said gaily.

"I didn't think a designer's work could be tiring," said Niels with a chuckle. "Don't you merely sit at a drawing board and doodle to your heart's content?"

Lars shook his head, frowning slightly. "Don't you believe it," he replied. "I'm involved in a new project for a company that's building a plant up near Gavle. That's about a hundred kilometers north of here," he added for Karen's benefit, "on the coast. It's going to be producing a wide variety of plastics, components for electronic assembly and so on." He wiped his hand across his forehead wearily. "There are several companies bidding on the job. A lot will depend on what I come up with. The right designs for the right price." He sighed. "It infuriates me sometimes how some people want to compromise quality for the sake of a budget."

"Who's building the plant?" asked Niels.

"The Lindstrom group," Lars told him. "They're just about the largest, but they're very cost-conscious."

"They have a good reputation," Niels comented.

"True, but they're difficult to deal with." He sighed again. "It would be so nice if I could just turn out my designs as I see fit, and not have to haggle with these executives whose only concern is a balance sheet, and with very little awareness of the technical specifications or scientific essentials."

"We've all got our problems," said Niels. "I've just gone through an aft·rnoon with some faculty members." He shook his head. "Like you say, it's difficult for some people to understand money cannot always be the bottom line."

"But it is, unfortunately. That's why there's been such a deterioration in American manufacture lately. Especially in their automobiles. Look at the number of cars being recalled for manufacturing defects. It's appalling, and the reason is cutting too many corners on the assembly line." His lip curled scornfully. "I pray we never get so slipshod over here."

Karen looked at Lars disbelievingly. She could scarcely believe that he could be so brutally tactless in front of her, knowing that she had only just arrived from the States, and was, in reality, American by birth as well as by instincts.

"I don't think you're being fair, Lars," she blurted out. "You know nothing about the manufacturing problems in the States."

"But I do, Karen. I know a great deal. And it isn't just what I read in the papers, either. On my visit to Chicago last week, I learned some grim details about the way big business is operating. Of course the general public isn't always aware of what goes on, just as you don't, obviously."

"My father dealt with some of the biggest farm equipment companies," Karen replied hotly, feeling almost insulted at his tone of voice, his condescending manner. "He seldom had problems, and his complaints about faulty manufacture were very few."

"Oh, I'm sure he didn't spill all those gory details at home," Lars said. "And you and your mother probably didn't show that much interest in his business affairs. Women seldom do," he added with a superior smirk at Niels, who chuckled knowingly.

"Business is a man's world, anyway," Niels said, puffing his pipe self-complacently.

"I think you're both being deliberately rude," Karen cried, unable to contain her mounting anger a moment longer. "Women play just as important part in business as men. There's hardly a job that a woman can't do just as well, if not better," she added tartly. "I was talking to Annabelle about this very subject this afternoon..."

"I'm sure you were," said Niels humorously. "It's her favorite basis for an argument."

"And I don't think your remarks about America were in good taste, either," Karen continued, her voice rising. "I may be settling in Sweden, but I'm still an American and very proud of it, too. And we still make the best cars in the world."

"That's your opinion," Lars retorted. "The facts prove otherwise. Why do you think European luxury cars outsell American two to one? It's the quality, the care we take over here."

"Well, obviously you don't care much about people's feelings." Karen felt her temper rising uncontrollably. "Even if you believe all that nonsense, you might have kept it to yourself instead of spewing it out in front of me. I don't appreciate it one bit."

Niels raised his eyebrows and exchanged a look with Lars. "Now, now, Karen, let's not get so upset," he said quietly.

"I'm sorry if I offended you, Karen," Lars said quickly. "I didn't mean to."

"Maybe so, but you should have thought of that."

"I said I was sorry."

"All right. Let's forget it, then. Just don't start running down my country."

"I won't, but don't you sell us short over here, either," he retorted; then his face broke into a smile. "Come on, have a glass of sherry with us. It'll soothe your nerves."

"My nerves don't need soothing, thank you. Besides, I think dinner's almost ready." She stood up and stormed into the kitchen, leaning up against the sink, biting her lips and feeling as though she were about to dissolve into tears. Annabelle looked at her for a moment, then came over to her, putting an arm around her shoulders.

"There, there, love," she whispered. "Chin up, now. You'll only spoil your digestion."

"It's already spoiled," Karen said tearfully. "In fact, this whole weekend's spoiled as far as I'm concerned. Oh, why did he say those things? And he's hardly looked at me since he arrived. He's just being... Ooooh!" She wiped her eyes and sniffed. "I wish he'd never come."

Annabelle smiled knowingly. "You'll feel better after dinner, and so will he," she murmured. "Now, come help me put the food on the table. Let's show 'em both what we women can do, eh?" She put a finger under Karen's chin and lifted it slightly. "Come on, Karen. No sense behaving like this."

"I know. I'm just being childish, but I can't help it." She reached for a tissue from the box on the counter, and blew her nose noisily. "All right. Let's get dinner over with."

Annabelle shook her head sadly and handed her the plate of broccoli. In silence they carried the dishes from the oven and set them in the center. Annabelle surveyed her efforts approvingly.

"A delicious looking meal, if I do say so myself," she said as Lars and Niels walked in. "Show me any man who could do as well," she added with a grin. "Come on, sit down. It's no good if it's cold."

Niels seated himself at the head of the table.

Lars sat down opposite Karen. Their eyes met for a second, and she looked down, spreading her linen napkin over her lap. Niels began carving the roast, and they began eating. Annabelle looked around, grinning.

"Now, come on, everyone," she said brightly. "This isn't a wake. Let's have a little cheerful chatter, shall we?"

Conversation was cordial, if sparse, and Karen concentrated on her food. Her anger had faded slightly, but she still felt a hard knot of resentment within her, not merely because of Lars' tactless remarks, but his seeming disregard for her. He could at least have said something when she met him at the door; or made some comment about how she looked. She had dressed especially to please him, and he had hardly looked at her. And she had been anticipating his visit so much... Well, it was all her own fault, she thought. She had built him up in her mind too much. He obviously regarded her as a young girl, immature and beneath his level of maturity. Maybe he was just playing with her after all. it was all very frustrating and confusing, and she wished the evening were over and he would just go back to Stockholm and never see her again...

CHAPTER 7

They were sitting in the livingroom, enjoying their coffee and some delicious tiny pastries that Annabelle had brought from her favorite Swedish bakery near the University. The dinner had been especially good and Niels and Lars were relaxed, almost boisterous, as they discussed the future of Sweden in the world market.

Karen wasn't sure whether it was the food or a resurgence of her feelings for Lars, but she did feel a dwindling of her anger. A certain reserve still lingered, but thanks to Annabelle's unflagging cheerfulness, Karen found herself joining in the conversation without any rancor over their earlier flareup; or, as she admitted to herself guiltily, over her childish display of sensitivity. Lars might have been a little more tactful in his comments, Karen thought, but she herself might also have kept her emotions in better check. After all, it wasn't so much what he said, but what he hadn't said that aroused her outburst. She had expected some indication of his feelings towards her—some little intimate word or look—instead of which he had arrived and settled down with as much warmth as he probably exhibited at one of his business conferences. But he had been tired, and now that he had eaten, recovered from the drive to Uppsala, and was feeling less tense, he would, she felt sure, be more like the Lars Tengborn she had been mooning over all week. And she had, she realized, built up their relationship into something far beyond the bounds of reason. However strongly they might feel for each other, the fact remained they were still comparative strangers who had met, traveled together, learned a little about each other and kissed once...certainly this was no basis for Karen to have let herself become so emotionally involved. They would have to get to know each other better, she knew, and she hoped this would happen as time passed; for she did like him.She liked him far too much considering the length of time she had known him.

"Sweden is really a world leader in design," Lars was saying. "Next to the Italians, I think we have the most progressive thinking, the most functional use of materials and the most modern styles. Look how our furniture is selling around the world. And how it is being copied, too," he added. "We have people coming here from all over—the United States in particular—to study our methods. Look at Vallingby and Farsta, too—outstanding examples of design skills in building community centers. I think you call them planned communities in America, Karen," he said, turning to her as he noticed her questioning expression. "We were one of the pioneers in the use of concrete and glass in building practical structures that are still highly aesthetic."

Niels nodded enthusiastically. "It is remarkable," he said, "the way we have forged ahead since the end of the war. Our industry has expanded enormously, our products sell well all over the world and you know what? I think it is because we have a particular design that appeals to people. A clean, functional look that is not only practical but beautiful."

Lars grinned. "It all gets back to the designers," he said triumphantly. "They say imitation is the sincerest form of flattery. You can see our designs being copied by countries everywhere, just as in America the Danish modern furniture was copied back in the Fifties, and is still very popular."

Annabelle winked at Karen. "It sure sounds like someone enjoys tooting his own horn," she said indulgently.

"And with good reason," said Niels. "Without the designers today, can you imagine what a hodge-podge of shapes there would be littering the landscape, to say nothing of the products in the stores? We should be thankful our country has produced men with the taste and imagination to be able to add beauty to our lives."

"And women, too, don't forget," Annabelle retorted with a grin. "To hear these two chatter on," she added to Karen, "you'd think it was men who are the only ones with taste and imagination."

"And before we get into that subject," said Lars, rising to his feet, "I think Karen and I had better take off."

Karen looked up at him, frowning. "Where to, Lars?"

"There's an exhibit at the Art Gallery," he said, looking at his wrist watch. "And we have about an hour and a half before it closes. I thought you might enjoy seeing it."

"Exhibit of what?"

"Industrial design, of course," he replied. "From Denmark. Furniture makers like Arne Jacobsen and Hans Wegner. And a lot more. It'll be interesting." He extended his hand and helped her up. "You may as well take a look at what Niels and I have been talking about. Improve your awareness of Scandinavia," he added with a twinkle in his eyes.

"Go on, Karen. You need to get out of the house," said Niels. "Besides, it'll give Annabelle and me a chance to go over a few things."

"All right. I'll be with you in a minute."

Karen went to her room, picked out a blue sweater to ward off the late evening chill, checked her makeup quickly, and then returned to the livingroom, feeling suddenly quite cheerful and happy. From the expression on Lars' face and his tone of voice, he was back to his usual self again: charming, appealing, attentive. She was not really interested in the exhibit, but felt it would be good to be alone with Lars, away from the slightly inhibiting presence of Niels and Annabelle. And once they were alone, she felt Lars might be more like himself again, shedding the superciliousness that surfaced whenever he seemed to be under some strain.

They said good-by to Niels and Annabelle, and climbed into the Volvo and were off in the direction of the university campus. Lars was humming to himself and Karen relaxed against the seat, her spirits almost back to the peak of pleasant anticipation she had experienced all day. All week, for that matter...

"You sound as though you're feeling better," she said.

He nodded. "Much, much better," he agreed brightly. "That dinner was wonderful. Annabelle certainly is a magnificent cook."

"That she is. Uncle Niels is lucky to have her around."

"Any man would be. Do you cook, by the way?"

"Oh, a little. Nothing spectacular, though." Karen laughed self-consciously. "I plan to get in lots of practice, though, once I get my own place."

"Oh." Lars looked at her curiously. "I thought you were going to live with your uncle."

Karen shook her head. "Oh, no. For the moment, of course, I'll be staying there. But I've been thinking about the future, and it just wouldn't be convenient, I believe. Not with Annabelle."

"Are they living together?"

"Good heavens, no! But I do think they'll wind up married pretty soon. At least that's the impression I get from Uncle Niels. Annabelle, of course, would like to have been married ages ago, from what he told me. But he's a little shy. He's lived alone so long."

"Yes, I can understand that. But I do think it's the only sensible thing for two people who care for each other."

"You've never thought of it yourself?"

"Many times, but I've never met the right girl." Lars looked at her for a brief moment. "That doesn't mean I'm a confirmed bachelor, though."

"I didn't think you were."

Lars laughed. "We have a few of those at the Center. Men who are so immersed in their work that they seldom think of anything else. I couldn't live like that. I enjoy my work, and I care a lot about it, but I still think one should have a balanced life: part work, part play. That's why I decided to come up this weekend, even though I was really bushed. I knew if I stayed in Stockholm, I'd probably wind up doing some studying, or even maybe going back to the office tomorrow."

"I'm glad you didn't. I've been looking forward to your visit all week."

"I have, too." He paused a moment. "I'm sorry about our little fracas earlier," he continued awkwardly. "I didn't mean to upset you."

"Let's forget it," Karen said briskly."It's over."

Lars chuckled. "At least it showed me one side of your nature."

"What do you mean?"

"That you're sensitive about a woman's role in society. And I think that's healthy, as long as you don't carry it too far, like some of these so-called liberated characters."

"To be quite honest, it wasn't that, nor what you said about America, which upset me. It was..." She paused, searching for words... "It was more the way you spoke, really." She glanced impishly at him. "That dreadfully superior look on your face, and your tone of voice. They just rubbed me the wrong way, I guess."

"Sorry about that. I do get a little snippy at times. You must forgive me, Karen. I wouldn't hurt you for the world, believe me."

"I know."

"In fact, you are rather special to me. I wouldn't have driven all this way if you weren't. I hope we can become very close in the future."

"I hope so, too, Lars. I like you very much."

"The feeling's mutual, I assure you."

They lapsed into silence, each knowing that to continue in such a personal vein would only lead to words that were premature and perhaps unnecessary; at least, for the moment. But Karen felt a warm glow again in her heart, reassured as she was by his statements. He did like her; time alone would tell exaclty how much, and for how long...

"Well, we're here."

She looked away from him to the cluster of buildings on their right, ivy-covered, thin-spired, traditional in their architecture. Above the doorway she could read a sign molded into the concrete: UPPSALA ART INSTITUTE.

They made their way inside, and Lars led the way through the wide, high-ceilinged lobby to a flight of stairs that took them up to the first floor gallery. A sign at the door announced: "EXHIBIT OF CONTEMPORARY DESIGN" printed in English and Swedish. A uniformed guard stood at one side, yawning. He glanced at them with a slight frown, came forward and spoke to Lars in Swedish. They exchanged a few words, then the guard laughed and moved back to his post.

"What did he say?" asked Karen.

"He told me the place is closing in forty-five minutes," replied Lars with a chuckle, "but he suspects we can see everything in fifteen. Obviously he isn't very impressed with the exhibit."

"He doesn't look the type who would be," said Karen. "Most security guards in the States are retirees, and not always very bright."

"Same over here," said Lars. "Anyway, let's go in here first," he indicated a room to their right, where interesting looking shelves hung from the ceiling, each containing an assortment of glassware, in many shapes, sizes and color. They made their way inside and Karen stopped, spellbound by the exquisite workmanship of the items—jugs, drinking glasses, bowls, tumblers, candle-sticks and platters. "Oh," she breathed, "these are fantastic."

"This display comes from the Orrefors Company," Lars said. "They're the most famous glass-blowing establishment in Sweden, with some of the top craftsmen in the country. They specialize in new and unusual shapes and colors for household items made of glass."

"Those salad bowls..." Karen pointed to a matching set of bright red oval dishes, each with a finely etched, fluted rim. "I've never seen anything so delicate."

"Delicate, but practical," said Lars. "You've seen Venetian glass, no doubt? Well, they make beautiful objects, but not very useful. You put them in a what-not cabinet to admire. The Orrefors Glass is meant to be used. That's often the basic idea behind much of Sweden's art—you can use it as well as admire its craftsmanship."

"I like it," said Karen, picking up a small vase and turning it to admire its spiral shape. "These all look clean and in keeping with today's lifestyle." She laughed. "My mother used to love that old-fashioned heavy cut-glass. On special occasions, she'd drag out the lace tablecloth, set the table with heavy, scroll-design silver and a big cut-glass bowl in the center with flowers. I guess it's all right if you like that sort of thing, but I felt it was too formal, too overpowering. It took half the enjoyment of a meal away because I was scared to death I might drop something and break it and then..." She sighed. "I really would have preferred eating with everyday dishes. I've never cared for what I call useless ceremony."

Lars nodded. "My parents were the same. In fact, they don't quite approve of many of my designs, nor of some of these..." He waved his hand at the exhibit as they moved back towards the door. "It's odd how older people cling so steadfastly to the old ways, the old things. But we have to move forward. It's a law of nature. I think that's why we're inspired to come up with new and different designs for the many things we use in our lives. Like furniture, for instance..."

They passed into the next room where chairs and tables were grouped in attractive settings. Lars hurried forward. "These are what really intrigue me," he said, his voice throbbing with excitement. "Arne Jacobsen. Hans Wegner. They've led the field for years. Just look at this chair. Isn't that exquisite?" He ran his hands over the wood, lovingly carved into a simple rounded shape, the grain glowing beneath the hand-rubbed finish. Karen nodded, her own enthusiasm prompted by Lars' obvious delight.

They passed through the furniture exhibit and on to an even larger room with ceramics, textiles and, at the far end, some miniature stage settings. Karen stood admiring some of the fabrics that were draped over stands. "These are really lovely," she murmured. "I'd love this for livingroom drapes," she added, feeling the texture of some material, roughly-woven with earth tones of orange, brown and yellow. Lars nodded.

"Most of this comes from Copenhagen," he said. "The designer, Bjorn Wiinblad, is a genius. He has a large studio there, and he produces mosaic tiles, ceramics, textiles—there's no limit to his creativity. He even does theatrical sets, like those over there." Lars pointed to the miniature sets that reminded Karen of the puppet shows she used to watch at the county fair in Minnesota. "And in case you're thinking men have the monopoly on all this, let me remind you of two of our greatest artists: Hjordis Hjalmarsdotter, and Gunilla Palmstierna. They both live in Stockholm and turn out some fantastic stuff—pottery and fabrics. Stockholm society women consider themselves truly well dressed if they have a couturier make up a dress from some of Hjordis' materials. And they're both relatively young women, too."

"I'm glad to hear that," said Karen, grinning at Lars' concern over her reactions. "It's like I said earlier: we women can hold our own in the design field. In any field, really."

"Maybe so," said Lars, putting his arm around her and guiding her back towards the main hallway, "but I still believe women are best at providing a home and children for a man. That's their basic role in life, after all."

"Agreed," said Karen, "but you can't stay pregnant and slaving over a hot stove forever."

"I should hope not." He laughed. "But then, spare time should be spent at something more than watching television." He paused a moment to gaze at a wall filled with graphic designs of machinery. "Hey, these are interesting. This is similar to what I do, Karen."

"They're beautiful," she said softly. "I don't know what they are, but they're very pretty."

Lars burst out laughing again. "This depicts the basic machine structure of a combine," he explained, pointing to the intricate series of lines. "You know, the things they use to harvest crops. Each one of these has to be carefully molded, machined and diecast for mass production. And a deviation of a few millimeters can cause the whole thing to fall apart. It's very complicated. I won't try to explain it."

"Don't. I'll take your word for it." They looked at each other, their eyes twinkling. "That's one thing I'll leave for the men to do," she added mischievously.

"I should hope so. It's like automobile design. That's a man's field exclusively. We have women who help with the artwork, but the basic designs are all done by men. It's the same everywhere, as far as I know."

Karen nodded. "I once went through the General Motors plant in Detroit. They said practically the same thing."

They moved on towards the main entrance as a warning bell sounded in the building. "Time to leave," said Lars with a smile. "And it looks like we're the last people here."

"I know. I was wondering where everyone is."

"The exhibit's been on for several weeks. I think most people who were coming have already been. I didn't want to miss it, though."

"I can understand why."

"Of course. Design is my life. I'm always interested in seeing what others are doing. Besides, it's only good business to keep up with the competition," he added with a dry chuckle.

"Tell me, Karen," he said as they walked down the steps and back to the car. "Don't you have any special interests, some hobbies, perhaps?"

"Not really." She settled in the front seat as he closed the door and went round to the driver's side and slid behind the wheel. "Anthropology is just about my chief goal in life, knowing all I can, learning everything that's possible. Which makes it a lifelong work, really."

"And your future plans? To teach at a university?"

The car pulled away from the sidewalk and headed back towards the edge of town. Karen thought for a moment. "I don't know," she answered truthfully. "I believe when the time comes, I'll be guided to whatever's best for me. Either a teaching position, or..." She shrugged. "Whatever."

"And if you get married, will that make a difference?"

"Of course it will. But I'm not counting on that. Marriage usually takes two, you know."

"I know only too well." He glanced at her quickly and saw the slight smile on her lips. "Come on, Karen. Be serious."

"I am, Lars. It will have to be a very special kind of man for me to marry. Someone who understands the fact that I am wrapped up in my studies, just like you're wrapped up in your work at the Center. Whoever I may marry one day, I hope he'll realize I'm not the type to settle down and start knitting baby clothes."

"You don't want a family?"

"Not yet. I think a family would be nice, but later on, when I've got my degree and spent a few years to get practical experience. Besides, I don't want to be tied down with children just yet. When I have any, I want to give them my total attention. Children are just about the biggest responsibility I can imagine for a woman."

"True. And I think you're wise. Besides, there're enough children in the world as it is."

"Oh. You sound as though you don't like children."

"Only when they're wanted by the parents, who in turn must be able to raise them properly, educate and care for them. My aversion to families is purely sociological. I spent three months once touring underprivileged countries—you know, Africa, India and the Middle East—and I saw the horrors that exist there. Babies crawling in the streets, untended, filthy, diseased. It's frightening. Yet some of these people go ahead breeding indiscriminately without any thought for what the results will be."

Karen nodded, impressed by the forceful tone in his voice, not mere academic condemnation, but a deep caring, a concern for humanity. She felt touched by his words. "It's sad, very sad. Which is all the more reason those of us who have better sense should take care not to add to the problem. Besides, if two people love each other enough to get married, their lives should be complete enough without desiring something more, like children."

"Some people may consider that a very selfish attitude."

"Not at all. I think it's a very considerate attitude. Look at Uncle Niels and Annabelle. Obviously they'll never have children, yet they enjoy a perfectly wonderful relationship. When they get married, as I'm sure they will be soon, they'll have everything two people could desire: mutual interests, a sharing of their individual pursuits, compatibility. And in their way, they'll contribute to the world through their academic achievements which, in all honesty, is a more significant contribution than merely producing a child."

"You do have a point," Lars agreed, chuckling softly. "I had no idea you were such a practical person."

"I am. Like I told you the other day, I'm not one of those scatter-brained girls you see in the movies."

"Hm...but you do have your immature moments, you must admit."

"Lars..." Karen looked at him disdainfully. "Let's not get into that again. Or are you spoiling for another argument."

"Never." He slowed down as they approached the house, then pulled up at the sidewalk and switched off the engine. "I wouldn't upset you again for the world. Not tonight, anyway," he added, leaning over and kissing her quickly on the cheek. "I don't want to get thrown out at this late hour. Now if you want to argue in the morning, fine. But then you could well talk your way out of a wonderful weekend in Stockholm I have planned for us."

She saw his eyes, very direct and sparkling in the dim light from the street lamp. "Oh, Lars..." She took his hand and squeezed it gently. "What do you have planned?"

"You'll find out tomorrow," he said mysteriously. "Come on, let's go in and see what those two lovebirds are doing."

They walked up the path and knocked at the door. Niels opened it and smiled broadly. "Back so soon?" he said loudly. "I thought you'd be gone till much later."

"Now whatever gave you that idea, Uncle Niels?" said Karen with a look of pretended innocence in her face as she walked into the house. They settled in chairs in the livingroom, and Karen looked around, frowning. "Annabelle not here?" she asked.

"No. She went home shortly after you left."

"Oh."

Niels raised an eyebrow and winked at Lars, who had taken out his cigarettes and was lighting one carefully. "I hope you didn't come back early hoping to catch me in the act of something indiscreet, surely?" he said with a chuckle.

"Uncle Niels!" Karen jumped to her feet again and started for the kitchen. "I'll put the water on for some tea. Would you all like that?"

"Good idea," said Niels. "Unless Lars would prefer a drink? I have some very excellent schnapps."

"No, tea will be fine."

Karen put the water on the stove and began getting the tea things ready on the table; then, changing her mind, she took a large tray down from the shelf and placed the cups, saucers on that instead; it would be nicer, she thought, having tea in the livingroom. It was so cozy, so homely with its rich looking furnishings and heavy drapes. She opened the cake tin and sliced some of the rich fruit cake that she had bought at the bakery that morning. She giggled to herself: quite the little homebody, aren't I? she thought. And why not? She was enjoying the role, not only because of Uncle Niels, but because of Lars. She wondered about their rather odd conversation in the car about families and children. His remarks had rather surprised her; she would have thought Lars the type to want a flock of kids, like so many Scandinavian families she had read about.

But then, she reminded herself: he was a career man, highly artistic and creative. He would want nothing to interefere with his work, to stifle his inspiration. Which was fine with her, because she had meant what she said about waiting a few years before having children. She had her interests that were all-important for the moment. And if she were to marry—to marry Lars, or anyone else—she would still want her career, her studies...

Marry Lars! She stopped still in the middle of

the kitchen, her eyes closed for a moment, imagining herself in a white bridal gown, walking up the aisle on Uncle Niels' arm, and Lars, in a formal suit, waiting for her, a soft, happy smile of welcome on his face... Oooh, what an enticing dream...

"The water's boiling!" She gasped, turned around as she heard Lars' voice. He was standing in the doorway, smoking his cigarette and gazing at her with a tolerant expression of amusement.

"Oh," she said, feeling slightly embarrassed. She turned and poured the water into the teapot. She raised her eyes and met his glance. "I'd love to know what you were dreaming about," Lars said.

"I'll never tell," said Karen, lifting the teatray and moving towards the door.

"Here, let me take that."

She handed Lars the tray and went back to the table for the plate of sliced fruitcake. As they approached the coffee table, Niels looked at them both with a knowing twinkle in his eyes.

"My, my," he observed humorously. "She's training you already, isn't she?"

"I'm not objecting," said Lars.

"That's enough out of you," Karen said pleasantly. "Both of you." She sat down and began pouring the tea. As she handed lars his cup,their eyes met and held, a firm, loving glance that was reassuring beyond words.

How wonderful to have him here, Karen thought: to be serving him, and later, if Uncle Niels trotted off to bed, they might cuddle up on the couch together...

She sat back, her heart beating faster at the thought, and began eating a slice of cake.

CHAPTER 8

Had Karen been able to order the morning, the mood and the magic of the moment, she could not have wished for anything better than she experienced as they drove from Uppsala to Stockholm. She felt almost euphoric, filled with an infinitely uplifting sense of joy as she leaned back against the soft leather seat of the Volvo and occasionally stole a glance at Lars behind the wheel, his strong hands guiding them at a moderate speed down the highway, his handsome profile silhouetted against the background of passing fields, trees and sun-drenched sky.

Of course, she had to admit, her happy state of mind stemmed from the previous evening with Lars, especially after Uncle Niels had conveniently gone to bed after tea, leaving them alone together. She had fully anticipated his suggesting they move to the wide, comfortable couch in front of the window, but instead he ambled over to Niels' favorite and well-worn armchair, dropped into it with a sigh of contentment and stretched out lazily.

Karen had cleared the tea things, then returned and, quite naturally, as though they had known each other for years, she dropped to the thick carpet and curled up at his feet like a worshipful puppy. He had asked if it would be all right if they had some music, which she readily agreed to, selecting an album of Beethoven sonatas from the impressive record collection above the stereo system. As she lay back, her head resting against his knees, his hand had strayed down and caressed her hair softly, his fingers occasionally tapping out the rhythm of the music.

They remained quiet, hardly talking, and allowed the soothing sounds to supplement their mood. Karen felt utterly at ease, and her earlier hope for some closer contact between them faded beneath the deeper rapport that engulfed them both.

When the record ended, Lars had stood up, helped her to her feet, embraced her briefly, kissed the top of her head and then begged off, pleading tiredness and an overpowering urge to crawl into bed and get some rest. She showed him to his room, and then, after putting out the lights, she had gone to bed herself, slipping between the sheets and falling asleep almost immediately. The minor disagreement before dinner was forgotten; as far as she was concerned, it had been an absolutely enchanting evening.

They had eaten breakfast with Niels, and then taken off for Stockholm. Karen had assured her uncle that she might not be back until the next day, and apart from a fleeting glance of apprehension, he had seemed reconciled to the arrangement. "Take care of her, Lars," he had said. "She's very special to me, you know."

Lars had nodded, understanding perfectly. "She's also special to me, sir," he had replied gravely.

And now they were on their way, with Karen looking forward to having a wonderful time, seeing the sights of Stockholm, enjoying the company which, she realized, was going to be the best part of it. Lars was obviously in a very good mood, totally recovered from his tiredness the night before.

"Ever heard of Gripsholm?" he asked her.

"No. What is it?" she asked impishly. "It sounds like an old man's disease."

"That's the grippe," he replied, chuckling. "No, this is the name of an enormous castle on the shores of Lake Malaren, near Stockholm. I plan to take you there this afternoon."

"Sounds like fun."

"It will be, I hope. With your interests, the castle shoud provide you with some interesting background information about Sweden."

"Is it very old?"

"Built in 1537, as I recall. It was the royal residence until the last century. Now it houses a large portrait collection. But the architecture is stunning."

"Good. I'll enjoy that. I love old buildings."

"Then I hope you're not too disappointed with Stockholm," Lars replied. "The city has its share of older structures, but at first glance, it looks more like a modern American city. You know, large concrete, steel and glass skyscrapers. Not as tall as New York or Chicago, certainly, but impressive."

"I'd rather see the older sections," said Karen.

"You will. I plan to show you everything I can. And, of course, I'm going to show you the Center where I work."

"You've never told me where you live, Lars," Karen said. "Or do you stay with your family?"

He laughed loudly. "Heavens, no! I left home about ten years ago. The family lives in Goteborg, anyway, much too far to commute, as my father foolishly suggested once. No, I used to have an older apartment not far from the Center, but a couple of years ago I moved to Farsta, one of our new planned communities. It's a suburb, but really more like a small city in itself. There's housing, parks, industry, shops—everything one needs, really. It's one of many similar communities that have been built to relieve the congestion in Stockholm, especially in the downtown areas. I love it there. It's like another world, really, with a much more relaxed atmosphere than Stockholm."

Karen nodded. "I can understand that. Our home in Minneapolis was quite a distance from the built-up area. In fact, we had about two acres around the house. It was so lovely. I had some very happy times in that house," she added nostalgically.

"What happened to it?"

"I sold it, just like I sold the business after my parents were killed. I felt it would be better for me to make a clean break. That's why I came over here. I could just as easily have continued going to school in the States, but when Uncle Niels wrote and asked me to move, I decided it was the ideal solution. It got me away from a lot of sad memories, and gave me the chance at a new life. I think it's been a wise decision for me."

Lars smiled at her. "I'm glad you did," he commented. "Just imagine, if you'd stayed over there, we might never have met."

"Would that have been so terrible?" asked Karen with a saucy grin in his direction.

"I would have survived," he replied imperturbably, "but not as happily, I feel sure."

"You'd have met some other girl."

"I'm sure, but not like you."

"And what's so special about me?"

"That, young woman, is something I will defer to a more appropriate time," he replied, grinning. "In any case, I'm sure you're quite aware of the answer."

"No, I'm not. But I'll look forward to hearing why I seem to have one up on Swedish girls. From those I've seen around Uppsala, they're beautiful."

"And you think you're not?"

Karen flushed. "I've never thought of myself that way."

"You are. Very lovely. Outside and inside," he added. "You see, I've learned one can get very tired of a pretty face unless there's more to the person. It's like you were saying last night about your uncle and Annabelle. It's compatibility that counts in the long run, not beauty." He glanced at her quickly. "You seem blessed in all areas, however."

"You're embarrassing me, Lars."

"Why? We're not afraid to admire the beauty of a painting, or some work of art, like we saw last night at the exhibit. So what's wrong in paying a compliment to a live work of art?"

"Just because..." She shifted in her seat, searching for the right words. She always felt so inadequate when trying to discuss her own merits. "Well," she ended lamely, "It doesn't leave me much to say, that's all."

"Then don't. Accept a sincere compliment graciously, because I do mean what I say. You're one of the few girls in my life who've had me lying awake at night, thinking about you. Like I told your uncle, you're something special, Karen."

She kept quiet, knowing that if she continued the conversation, her voice might easily give away the mounting emotion within her. But still, she wondered, if he feels so strongly about me, why hasn't he showed it more? Why did he give her that brief, almost fatherly kiss last night? She had fully expected him to embrace her and kiss her on the lips; not once, but many tmes. Perhaps, she reasoned, he was inhibited because they were in her uncle's house. Or, on the other hand, he might not have wanted to start anything to arouse his passions and then have to stop, frustrated and yearning for a consummation of their feelings that he knew would be impossible at the moment. Obviously he was traditional enough in his attitudes not to attempt anything before they could carry it to its natural conclusion; he had given her the impression he regarded marriage as the only logical and acceptable way to a woman's heart...

But again, she would undoubtedly find out more about his true intentions this weekend; for if they were staying over in Stockholm, as they probably were, would he suggest she spend the night with him at his apartment? Or maybe he would take her to a hotel...or perhaps to a girl friend's house? The intriguing alternatives flashed through her mind, giving her a delicious tingle of anticipation, if not a certain apprehension. He would certainly not force himself upon her, she knew, but she was more afraid of her own feelings than his. If there were to be any danger, it would not be from him, but from her own burgeoning desires to hold him, to feel his strong arms around her... Stop it! She knew if she let her mind wander into those forbidden areas, she would only cloud the carefree feelings they shared. Let it be, she thought firmly, let things fall into place at the right time. There was only one thing to concentrate on now: the scenery, and the sights of Stockholm, which, she realized, they were approaching.

Among the cluster of apartment houses and industrial structures, Karen saw a curious sight: a large ferris wheel, a roller-coaster and various other rides to be found at a carnival. She pointed to it and asked Lars: "What an odd place for an amusement park." He nodded. "We have several all over the city," he told her. "And they're not just for the rides and all that nonsense. They hold concerts there occasionally. You've heard of the singer Birgit Nilsson?" Karen nodded. "She was born on a farm not far from here, and often gives a concert, right there at that amusement park. Just herself and a pianist, but then with that voice of hers, who needs an orchestra?"

"How odd. I'd have thought she would have stuck to opera."

"For her professional appearances, she does. But she has always believed in sharing her talent with everyone, not merely opera lovers. So she comes to parks and smaller gatherings and sings. I think it's a wonderful gesture on her part."

"It certainly is," Karen agreed. "She must be a wonderful person."

"It stems from our national belief," Lars continued. "We have always felt that individual talents are part of everyone's heritage. They are to be shared, enjoyed by the masses. We work hard, but we also play hard. Industry has made great strides in this country, but so has art and culture. Our playwrights, our cinema producers and directors like Ingmar Bergman, and many others—they have all helped to spread appreciation of art throughout the land; throughout the world, for that matter. There...look!"

He slowed down as they swung into a wide four-lane freeway leading to the downtown area of Stockholm. Clusters of large, twenty-storey modern buildings could be seen ahead, their pale blue and white walls rising starkly into the sky.

"We're entering the busiest part of the city now," Lars explained, and Karen noted a ring of pride in his voice. "You see all the modern high-rises there? They all have underground floors for parking and deliveries. No stopping is allowed on the streets because of the congestion. It's an excellent plan, really. It keeps traffic moving and makes the streets safer for pedestrians."

"Everything is regulated, controlled?"

"Yes, for the most part, I'd say so. But that's where the planning has benefited us. We design our cities just like we design our products: for beauty as well as their practical application. You'll see the best example in Farsta, where I live. It's an ideal community, built from the ground up, with everything planned for the greatest convenience and use of space and energy."

Lars swung the car off the street and into an archway leading down below street level. He parked the car and they made their way up to the crowded sidewalk. Karen stood a moment, gazing around spellbound. "I had no idea..." she began, but Lars guided her forward before she could verbalize the wonder she felt at the city...the mixture of older shops and stores and the new, modern buildings, their clean, graceful lines in harmony with their surroundings despite the essentially progressive flavor of the architecture.

"That's the Stockholm Concert Hall," Lars pointed across the street to a wide, massive structure in front of a cobble-stoned area with benches surrounding a group of statues. In answer to her unspoken question, Lars explained: "The grouping there is by Carl Milles. The tall statue in the middle is Orpheus, the mythological musician. It's one of his most famous and, I believe, just about the best example of his work."

They walked across, making their way through the busy noontime crowds, and Karen stood, gazing up at the exquisite work of art that towered, she estimated, at least thirty feet above their heads. "It's beautiful," she whispered. "You know something? It reminds me of you."

Lars burst out laughing. "How can you say that?" he teased her. "You've never seen me without my clothes."

"Oh, you're terrible," she chastised him, trying unsuccessfully to stifle a grin.

"Come on, I want to take you to the Center," Lars said. "It's not too far. You don't mind a walk, do you?"

"Not a bit. I love walking."

They turned and started down the sidewalk. At the end of the block, they turned right and Karen found herself looking down a long, tree-lined avenue, with ancient apartment houses flanking the busy thoroughfare. At the end, a gleaming modern building in blue and black rose like a symbol of progress into the sky.

"That it?"

Lars nodded. "Yes. And way up there, on the fourteenth floor, is where I slave each day for thirty pieces of silver."

"And," Karen added knowingly, "to make your mark in the world."

"True."

They strolled by the scrubbed brick terraces outside the stores and restaurants that comprised the ground floor of the buildings. Again, Karen noted the appealing mixture of old and new: cafes with wicker chairs and tables filled with Swedes enjoying their lunch, and above their heads, suspended on a modernistic chrome scaffolding, were the frosted white lamps, looking like flattened ballons. "People parade along here until quite late at night," said Lars. "I sometimes have dinner here and sit, watching the crowds."

"It's very picturesque," Karen observed. "Almost like the sidewalk cafes in Paris that I've heard about."

"Exactly. We Europeans prefer to eat outdoors, really, as long as the weather permits."

"It's charming. I've often wondered why American restaurants didn't follow suit years ago."

"Because," Lars said, not unpleasantly, "your people have always tried to be different, even though their way isn't always better. In any case, if America were a carbon copy of Europe, we'd lose out on all that wonderful tourist traffic each year."

Karen decided to ignore his remarks, not wanting to start another argument between them. She was too enraptured by the feeling of total abandon prompted by the excitement of visiting a new place, seeing new faces—especially the happy faces of the Swedes as they scurried to and fro along the streets, doing their weekend shopping or relaxing on the numerous benches on the sidewalk, enjoying the brilliant sunshine.

They reached the entrance to the Wenner-Gren Administrative Center. "Would you like to come up to my office?" asked Lars.

"Not today," replied Karen, staring up at the monolithic structure towering above their heads. "Maybe some other time. I'd rather go on and see what else there is. Office buildings..." She shrugged. "Unless you want to go up, of course. Do you?"

"Oh, I thought I might check my desk for mail.

I'm expecting some papers about this new contract we're bidding on. Would you mind?"

"Of course not. I just didn't want you to feel you should because of me. I can see the inside anytime."

"All right. Come on."

They walked into the spacious lobby, plain, stark but nonetheless impressive in its functional beauty. Lars led the way to the elevators and they rode up with quiet speed to the fourteenth floor, down a series of corridors and into an office. Karen walked over to the outside wall, which was glass from floor to ceiling. She looked out and gasped. "Oh, what a glorious view," she murmured. "You must feel truly inspired working in here."

Lars nodded. "I enjoy it," he admitted, riffling through a handful of envelopes on a desk. "Well, it's not here. I guess they haven't sent it yet."

"Was it important?"

"Any contract is important in this business. No matter. It will probably come on Monday." He walked over to her. "Now, you get just as good a view from here as you would from the plane. Better, really, because you can see more." He pointed to the west. "You see way out there in the distance? That area of water? That's part of Lake Malaren, where I'm taking you today."

"Oh, then it isn't far?"

"Not really, although the lake extends for fifty or sixty kilometers inland. It's a series of inlets, little islands and small peninsulas. Almost an inland ocean, really. Sweden has many similar areas up and down the coast."

"Like Minnesota," said Karen. "They call that the land of the lakes. It's a fabulous tourist area in the summer."

Lars nodded. "The same over here. Only Sweden is a little larger than Minnesota," he added with a smile. "Come on, I think we'd better be making tracks if you're going to see Gripsholm Castle today. It's not far, really, but it takes a while to go through it."

They left the office, and as they were walking back towards the elevators, a voice rang out down the corridor.

"Lars Tengborn! Don't tell me you're working Saturdays?"

They stopped, and Lars turned and looked at the tall figure which had just emerged from a doorway. Karen noted, with a sudden twinge of curiosity, that Lars' instinctive smile faded when he saw the man's face, and a steely look of appraisal spread over his features. The man approached them, and Karen couldn't help feeling a surge of admiration for his finely chiseled face, his penetrating dark brown eyes and his impressive build. For a moment she found her mind rushing back to high school, and she thought: this could be Kevin, slightly older, more mature, more sure of himself...

"Hello, Gunnar," said Lars. "I'd like you to meet Karen Christensen. I was just showing her the office." His voice was almost formal, and Karen got the distinct impression that Lars did not care for the man. "Karen, this is Gunnar Lindstrom."

"How do you do?" he greeted her, his rich voice vibrating with genuine pleasure as he extended his hand and took hers firmly. "Don't tell me you're Lars' new assistant?"

Karen shook her head. "No. Just a friend," she replied.

"Pity. This building could stand a few more beautiful women on its staff. Although your last helper wasn't bad at all, Lars. Whatever happened to her, by the way?"

"You mean Signe?" asked Lars. "She left to get married."

"Oh. Well, your loss is somebody's gain, I suppose," said Gunnar. "If I were you, I'd try and get Miss Christensen to come to work for you. I know I would."

"I'm sure," said Lars curtly. "It so happens Karen's an archeology student. I don't think she plans to take up office work."

Gunnar's eyes widened. "Archeology, eh? You and good old King Gustaf of Sweden? That's a very studious pursuit for such a lovely young lady."

"Do you work here yourself?" asked Karen, anxious to get the subject off herself. She was beginning to feel uncomfortable, the way he was staring at her with such brashness, such lascivious appraisal.

"Oh, no." Lindstrom laughed broadly. "I'm just visiting."

"On a Saturday?" Lars' voice was brisk, and his eyes were openly suspicious as he gazed at the other man.

"Yes. I was supposed to meet Frederick here and go over some papers," Gunnar answered smoothly. "I expect he's held up in traffic. He'll probably be along shortly."

Lars took Karen's arm and nodded to Gunnar. "We must be going," he said shortly.

"Of course, I didn't mean to delay you. Nice meeting you, Miss Christensen." He bowed his head slightly, and Karen felt his eyes fasten mockingly on her. "And you, too, Lars. I'll probably see you around next week."

"Nice meeting you," Karen murmured.

They entered the elevator, and only after the doors closed did Lars give an explosive sigh. "I'd like to know what he's doing here," he said angrily.

"Isn't he suppose to be in the building?"

"No, he isn't."

"Who is he, Lars?"

"He's the son of one of our leading industrialists. And a real shady character, too. He has quite a reputation."

"With the ladies, no doubt," said Karen with a giggle. "The way he looked at me, I felt undressed."

"I know. I can't stand him, to be quite honest. I'd still like to know what he's up to."

They reached the ground floor and made their way back to the car. After a minor traffic jam, Lars managed to reach the outer highway and they were soon moving quickly along the edge of Lake Malaren, away from the frantic confusion of downtown Stockholm.

"Is it far to the castle?" Karen asked.

"Not very. We should be there in a half hour or so."

She relaxed in the seat, taking in the countryside which, like the land between Stockholm and Uppsala, was flat, heavily wooded and lush with leafy trees and open, fertile fields. And while the scenery held her attention, she found her mind flitting back to Gunnar Lindstom. It was amazing how much he resembled Kevin. The same dark good looks, thick black hair and the muscular build of a football player. She wondered whether

Kevin had grown up to look like this. If he had, he was probably even more of a Lothario than he had been in high school; which is what Gunnar was, according to Lars' brief but explicit comment. Maybe it was just pure masculine jealousy. After all, Gunnar was extemely virile looking, his face exuding sex appeal. Lars, on the other hand, was equally handsome, but in a more aesthetic way. They were, Karen realized, exact opposites...

"Well, there it is." Lars' voice broke into ther reverie and she looked ahead and gasped with delight.

"It's like a fairy-tale castle," she exclaimed.

As the car approached the grounds, Karen let her eyes linger on the ancient building, its spires rising, she estimated, at least sixty or seventy feet in the air, looking almost like the minarets on the Taj Mahal. The main body of the castle was only six, maybe seven storeys high, but the four circular buttresses on each corner rose majestically another twenty or thirty feet.

Lars pulled up at the entrance and they climbed out, pausing a moment to savor the majesty of the castle. Karen pictured kings and queens in their royal robes, descending the steps to enter their horse-drawn carriages, while a retinue of velvet-clad attendants stood respectfully to attention on each side of the front door.

"Oh, I'm going to enjoy this," she said ecstatically, taking Lars' arm and moving up the steps with him.

"I'm glad," he murmured. "I hope there'll be many things we can enjoy together."

"There will be," she replied.

CHAPTER 9

The dinner had been simple, but delicious. Lars had taken Karen to what he called his favorite little Swedish restaurant in Farsta, a short distance from his apartment. The owner was a big, blustery woman who reminded Karen of Annabelle, but without the latter's sophistication and sense of humor. The meal had been served with almost military precision by two girls in stiffly starched aprons, both obviously terrified of their employer, who stood at the kitchen door, directing operations in a stentorian voice and punctuating her commands with a wave of a wooden spoon. Karen observed the proceedings, trying hard not to giggle, and only after she and Lars were left alone in their corner of the room, did they both collapse into helpless laughter. "She is a character," Lars said, "but she's the best cook I know of. I've been coming here for over a year now."

"She's marvelous," Karen said. "She reminds me of Brunhilde doing the Ride of the Valkyries, or whatever that is...you know what I mean?" Lars nodded, and admitted he had often pictured her the same way. Their laughter subsided and they sat, staring at each other in the soft light.

"This has been such a wonderful day," Karen said finally.

"It has. I feel so relaxed now I could fall asleep right here."

"You mean you're not taking me dancing?"

"I wasn't planning it, unless you insist."

"What if I do?"

"Then I expect I'll be forced to." His eyes twinkled. "But I don't think you'd be quite that demanding, would you?"

"Demanding?" Karen tossed her head in mock annoyance. "I get invited for the weekend and my host poops out on me at...let me see...nine-thirty. Of course," she added with an impish grin, "you can go back to your apartment and give me the car. I'm sure I'd find someone only too happy to take me dancing at a disco."

"Disco?" Lars gazed at her in horror. "I can imagine nothing more revolting, frankly. And I certainly wouldn't let you drive my car."

"Now you're sounding like Uncle Neil. He considers disco a despicable return to primitive mating rituals."

"He's right. When I dance, I like to hold a girl in my arms, move gently and feel her pressing against me. Disco isn't quite my speed. I'm the romantic type," he added, his mouth twitching humorously.

"I had a feeling you were. And I also have a feeling you have just the right kind of music at your apartment, and perhaps a little patio where you'll have a bottle of wine and two glasses..." She raised an eyebrow and looked at him knowingly.

"Would that be so contrary to your expectations?" Lars asked.

"No." Karen hesitated a moment. "But a *tete-a-tete* like that can have regrettable consequences, especially when the two people involved let themselves get carried away. And I have no intention of being seduced, no matter how the idea might appeal to you."

"For your information, I didn't bring you to Stockholm to assault your virtue," Lars said bluntly. "And whatever happens, I hope we are both mature enough to handle ourselves with restraint."

Karen burst out laughing again. "Oh, Lars, you sounded so stuffy. Just like Uncle Niels."

His smile faded somewhat. "I'm getting a little weary of being compared with your uncle," he said dryly. "There does happen to be about twenty-five years difference in our ages."

"So? There happens to be about ten years difference in your age and mine," Karen said quickly. "I don't think age has anything to do with how people get along."

"True, but you're intimating I'm as stuffy as your uncle."

"I'm not. I just said you sounded like him."

"Same thing, really." He sighed and signalled the waitress for the check. "Anyway, I frankly don't feel up to dancing tonight. Maybe we can have an early night and be fresh in the morning. I have some interesting things planned for you tomorrow," he added, his voice taking on a slightly forced enthusiasm. Karen stared at him, frowning. She recognized the tightness around his mouth, the beginnings of a supercilious tone to his words.

"I have a spare bedroom in my apartment," Lars continued, "but if you feel you'd prefer it, I can take you to a little hotel around the corner." He saw her expression of disappointment, almost disbelief. "The spare room locks from the inside, by the way."

"Oh, Lars, stop it." Karen's spirits plummetted suddenly and she felt unless she brought things back to their previous level of easy, carefree enjoyment, the evening could well wind up a disaster. She forced herself to smile,and reached for his arm, squeezing it tenderly. "Why is it we seem to slide into agruments at the drop of a careless remark? Come on, we're having a wonderful time. And I'm not upset at not going dancing. And I'm not afraid to spend the night in your apartment, either. So don't make a Federal case out of it, please." He pursed his lips; then slowly his face relaxed.

"I'm sorry. I know I can be an awful bore sometimes. Thank you for pulling me up. I don't want to spoil the evening, believe me."

"You haven't. Now come on, let's go back to your place and maybe have a cup of tea and talk before going to bed. You do have tea, I presume?"

Lars smiled. "Of course."

He paid the bill and they left the restaurant, walking out into the cool night air. Karen stood still, closing her eyes and taking a deep breath. "Ooooh," she sighed. "The air smells so good."

"That's why I moved out here," said Lars, taking her arm and starting to walk back towards the car. "I get enough smog each day at work. Out here, we have hardly any pollution."

"Talking of work, that reminds me," said Karen, falling into step with him. "You remember that man we met at the Center today? What was his name?"

"Gunnar Lindstrom." Lars made a face. "Not my favorite person at all. What about him?"

"Well, he said something about your hiring me as your assistant. Are you really needing someone?"

"Well, yes. Signe was with me over a year, then she left. Got married to one of the designers on my floor. I was happy for her, but it sure left me out on a limb."

"All right, how about me?"

"I don't follow you."

"Well, you know we've been talkig about my getting a job. Getting an apartment of my own."

"I thought you were going back to school."

"I am, but not until the fall semester. I think it would be only sensible to get a job so I could have something to do the next two months."

"Oh, I see. Well, frankly, I don't want someone who's only going to stay a few months. In any case, I don't think you're properly qualified. My assistant has to have some knowledge of graphics, art and all that." He grinned at her. "That's a long way from your favorite subject, isn't it?"

Karen chuckled. "You mean the girl you hire has to be able to draw, or sketch?"

"No, but...well, Karen, to be honest, I don't think it would be anything that would interest you."

"On the contrary, it interests me very much. And there's something you don't know about me."

"Like what?"

"Like my five years of art. My undeniable skill with the pencil." She suppressed a giggle as she saw the amazement cross his face. "I can also type fifty words a minute and take fair shorthand. I worked for my father three summers in a row as secretary."

"Well, I'll be darned." Lars stopped, swung her around and stared at her with a soft smile. "It sounds like you could well be qualified."

"I have many hidden talents, Mr. Tengborn," she replied saucily, looking up into his eyes.

"No." He shook his head and resumed walking. "I don't think so. If you were to come to work, I'd only have to hire someone else when you go back to school. That means going through it all over again. Sorry, Karen."

"You'll be sorrier if you wind up with some goggle-eyed girl who can't tell a blueprint from a silver print. Or who can't tell a line drawing from a photostat." She laughed at the dumbfounded expression on his face. "Am I convincing you? I mean, there'll be very little training, I'm sure. So you wouldn't be wasting time. You can save all that for whoever replaces me in the fall."

"Let me think about it."

"Okay. I'll give you five seconds."

He laughed. "Karen, you're impossible. Impossibly delightful," he added. "All right. I know I'm sticking my neck out, but I'm willing to give it a whirl. On one condition, though."

"What's that?"

"If you don't cut it after a few days, you mustn't be upset if I let you go."

"Of course not. Let's say I'll come to work on a week's trail basis. Fair enough?"

"Fair enough." They reached the car and Lars unlocked the door for Karen to slide into the passenger seat. He went around and got behind the wheel. "You're quite sure, Karen? I mean, you haven't even asked what sort of salary we pay."

"I'm not doing it for the money, Lars," she replied frankly. "I have more money than I'll ever spend in my lifetime. I need the job to help me adjust to this country, to the people. And to improve my Swedish, which is pretty bad."

"Okay. You're on." He started the car and they moved down the street. Karen felt a wild exultation in her heart. She would be working with him, which meant they would be together eight hours a day; and knowing how he felt about her, they would undoubtedly eat together, probably go out most evenings together... It wouldn't only be her knowledge of the language that would improve, but her knowledge of Lars Tengborn. And most certainly after the summer was over, she would know for sure how she felt about him; and how he felt about her. And by that time, who could tell what might develop...

They drove back to Lars' apartment, and he showed her into the spare room. Like the entire place, it was tastefully furnished with modern style furniture and modernistic paintings on the wall, together with some framed designs of his own creation. Despite the lack of traditional touches, the apartment had a warmth to it, a pleasant ambiance that set Karen's apprehensions to rest. Not that she had expected the usual esoteric bachelor pad; but the absence of garish touches was a welcome relief, and signalled Lars' innate sense of decor and a good sense of style and color. She had always felt a home reflects the owner's character, and judging from the apartment, Lars was conservative, reliable but still not without the occasional sparkle of humor and mischief. She felt at ease, and after they had a quick cup of tea, they both retired for the night. As she closed the door to the spare room, she stared for a moment at the key in the lock; then, deciding that preparedness was the best insurance against temptation, she quietly turned the key. She heard Lars putting out the lights in the livingroom and retiring to his room. She lay awake a few minutes, thinking over the events of the day—the enthralling visit to the Gripsholm Castle, the dinner and her decision to start work at the Center; then, without realizing it, she fell asleep.

She awoke to the tantalizing smell of bacon frying. She quickly dressed, and joined Lars in the small kitchen. He was dressed in jeans and a close-fitting knit shirt and she was amazed at his build: lean, wiry but well muscled. He greeted her warmly, and asked her to pour the coffee, which was perking noisily on the table.

She sat down and grinned at him. "This is what I call service," she commented. "Do you treat all your overnight guests this way?"

"But of course. If they like the service, they come back."

She watched as he drained the bacon on a paper towel, then broke four eggs into the pan and scrambled them quickly. He took a tray of pastries out of the oven, and served the meal. They ate in relative silence, and then, having put the dishes in the sink, Lars relaxed with his coffee, smoking a cigarette and looking at Karen with a quizzical expression.

"So you want to come and work for me?" he said.

She nodded. "I meant it, Lars."

"Then you'll have to get a place in Stockholm. You can't drive back and forth from Uppsala every day."

"Of course."

"When do you want to start?"

"Whenever you want me to. Tomorrow, maybe?"

"Very well. Then we'll have to find you an apartment today."

Karen glanced around the room. "You know, something like this would suit me very nicely. Do you think they have any vacancies?"

He chuckled. "I'm way ahead of you," he said

with a smile. "I called the manager this morning. She has a one-bedroom available, just two doors up the street."

"Oh, that's wonderful. Is it furnished?"

"No, but they can supply furniture if you want it."

"That would be fine. Can we go see it?"

"Of course, when we've finished our coffee."

Karen leaned forward excitedly. "I can't wait. This is all so thrilling. I wonder what Uncle Niels will say."

"He'll be disappointed, but I don't think he'll ry to dissuade you."

"No, he wouldn't do that. Besides, I'll be close enough to see him and Annabelle often. Maybe on weekends."

"Of course. There are many spots I want to show you, and we go through Uppsala on the way."

"You sound as though you plan to monopolize my weekends." Karen eyed him steadily, her chin tilted as she smiled provocatively.

"Why not? You don't know anyone else in Stockholm."

"Oh, but give me a few days, and I'm sure I'll have all the offers I can handle," she answered coyly.

"I have no doubt of that, though I suspect any offers you get will not be the kind you'll welcome."

"You let me worry about that. I can handle just about anything."

He laughed. "That remains to be seen. Anyway, you'll find me a very jealous person. I'm always that way with someone I care about."

"Oh." Their eyes met and she put out her hand to touch his arm. "I care about you, too, Lars, but I don't want to be tied down. Not just yet. You understand?"

"Yes, and I don't want you to feel obligated to go out with me. In fact, there may be many times I won't be able to. This contract I'm working on, you know..." He sighed impatiently. "It's geting near the deadline for submission. I may have to work some evenings, even a weekend." He stood up and carried their cups to the sink. "So just let's see how things go."

"Right. And now I want to go see this vacant apartment."

As they walked down the street, Karen was amazed at the number of people, not only out walking, but driving. "do all Swedes get up early on Sunday mornings?" she asked.

"With weather like this, we like to enjoy as much of it as we can. We don't get that much sun, you know. It's a luxury for us." They stopped in front of a small apartment unit halfway down the street. "This is it," said Lars, pointing to the windows on the first floor. "The end one, overlooking the park."

"That's the vacant apartment?"

"Yes. And believe you me, you'll be lucky to get it. Farsta is famous for having very few empty houses or apartments. It's the best suburb in the city, really. Higher class people, and lots of open space between the buildings. The park over there is the largest. It has a wonderful lake with boats. And a marvelous swimming pool, too. Plus a big recreation hall where they hold dances twice a week. This is really a lovely place to live."

"I can imagine."

He led the way to the manager's office on the ground floor, and introduced Karen to Mrs.

Nansen, a homely, middle-aged woman with a broad smile and a very friendly manner. "American?" she asked. "Well, we'll have to make you feel welcome, won't we, Lars?" She took Karen's arm and guided her up the stairs to the end of the building. "This is truly one our nicest apartments, my dear. It has the view of the park, and it also has a corner exposure. You get breezes from the north and the west. Very airy and sunny. I know you'll enjoy living here."

"And you do supply furniture?" Karen asked, staring around the empty room. Mrs. Nansen nodded. "Of course, if you want it. We have many nice styles you may choose from in our warehouse."

Karen walked slowly through the rooms, not unlike the small apartment she had rented while attending Northwestern University in Chicago. The livingroom was fairly spacious, with a wide fireplace at one end, framed with dark red bricks that contrasted warmly with the cream-colored walls. The bedroom was fairly small, but with two spacious closets and a small bathroom. The kitchen was compact but with an electric range and a refrigerator.

"This is lovely," she said, beaming delightedly. "I'll take it."

"I knew you'd like it," Lars said happily.

"Good. And there is no lease," Mrs. Nansen said. "You just pay by the month. When would you want to move in, my dear?"

"Today," said Karen, her eyes sparkling with excitement.

"You certainly make up your mind in a hurry, don't you?" said Lars.

"Why not? If I'm starting work for you tomorrow, I'd better be moved in by then."

"Very well." Lars grinned tolerantly. "I suppose I can drive you up to Uppsala and get your things."

"Of course you can," said Mrs. Nansen. "You can be back by nightfall. Maybe you two would like to share our dinner with us?" She patted Lars on the arm. "This young man is one of my favorite tenants," she added, winking at Karen. "And now he had himself a girl-friend...well, I must make you both feel at home."

Karen flushed. "That's awfully good of you, but you don't have to.."

"Enough!" Mrs. Nansen held up a hand to silence the polite refusal that was forming on Karen's lips. "It will be my pleasure to have such a charming young lady at my table. Call it Swedish hospitality, if you like."

Lars shrugged his shoulders. "You can't argue with her," he said resignedly. "Besides," he added with a grin, "Mrs. Nansen is a wonderful cook."

"Oh, go on!" Mrs. Nansen blushed delightedly and led the way downstairs to the warehouse at the rear of the building. Karen selected a couch in deep earth tones of brown and gold, together with a matching armchair and a selection of end tables and a large coffee table with a built-in planter at one end. For the dining area, she chose a chrome and plate glass table and chrome chairs with dark brown canvas seats and backs.

"I think that should be enough," she said, remembering that the apartment was not very large.

"What about the bedroom?" Mrs. Nansen said. "You'll need a dressing table and, of course, a bed." She raised her eyebrows. "You'll be needing a double bed, no doubt?" she said with a meaningful glance at Lars.

"I think a single bed would be better," Karen replied quickly. It'll give me more room in there."

Mrs. Nansen chuckled. "Suit yourself. Personally, I like more room in the bed than around it."

"That's enough out of you," said Lars pleasantly, and they both broke into loud laughter, and Karen looked shyly away, realizing that Mrs. Nansen was presuming more to her relationship with Lars than actually existed, but she decided not to make an issue of it. It was none of the woman's business, anyway...

They returned to the office and Karen paid for her first month's rent, and then she and Lars began their drive back to Uppsala.

"Uncle Niels will certainly be surprised," Karen said gaily as they sped down the broad highway heading north out of Stockholm.

"I hope he won't get the wrong idea," said Lars.

"Meaning what?"

"Meaning that I've set you up in an apartment," he replied with a grin. "You know Mrs. Nansen thinks that we're lovers."

"I got that impression," Karen responded, "but in her line of work, I guess she takes that for granted."

"True. There are many unmarried couples living in that area. She doesn't care, really; she's just curious, like most gossipy old women. I am a little concerned about your uncle, however."

"You leave him to me," said Karen confidently. "He knows I don't plan to live with him indefinitely. We talked about it this week, and he agreed it might be better, especially with his situation with Annabelle. He likes his privacy, which I can understand."

"Maybe so, but you've only been here less than a

week."

"Don't worry, Lars. He's not going to object. How can he? I'm over eighteen."

There was comparatively little traffic on the highway and before long, they had pulled up in front of Niels' home. There was another car parked outside. "Annabelle must be here," Karen said as they climbed out and hurried up the garden path. They walked in and saw Niels and Annabelle seated on the couch, reading.

"Welcome home," said Niels, rising and giving Karen a hug.

They settled down and Karen told them the news. Annabelle's face glowed with joy, but Niels looked quite disappointed.

"I knew you would leave eventually," he said sadly, "but I never thought it would be this soon, Karen."

"Oh, hush!" Annabelle waved a hand at him perfunctorily. "I think it's fantastic. She's got a job, a place of her own and in one of the nicest sections of Stockholm. What more could she ask for?"

"I suppose so," said Niels gloomily.

"And I'll be seeing you often," Karen reassured him. "Lars says there're many places he wants to take me, and they're all north of here. So I'll probably be back next weekend, at least to see you for a little while." She looked impishly at Annabelle. "And to have one of your famous dinners, perhaps?"

"Of course, my dear, of course."

Karen packed her belongings and helped Lars load them in the back of the Volvo, and after an affectionate farewell, they took off, back to Stockholm. The sun was setting and the landscape was a soft mixture of deepening blue and gray as twilight descended. Karen stared out the window, feeling elated, but at the same time, a little sad. Uncle Niels had looked so forlorn as he stood at the gate and waved them good-by. No matter. She would be back, and in the meantime, she would be settling down to her new life, in her own apartment, and the next day she would be starting her new job.

"Oh, Lars," she said fervently. "I feel so terribly happy. Excited and happy."

"I'm glad," he replied, giving her a quick sidelong glance. Their eyes met and Karen reached over and squeezed his arm. No words were necessary at that point. In silence they sped on through the gathering darkness.

CHAPTER 10

After a week of working at the Wenner-Gren Center, Karen felt she had been there all her life. Not only did she slip easily and quickly into the routine of the office, but she found, to her amazement (and Lars' joyful amusement) that her knowledge of Swedish was improving daily, with her slipping back into the language with very little effort. "My parents used to speak it when I was a child," she explained to Lars. "I expect it's just all coming back to me now."

They dined together on the Saturday evening, and Lars gave her the news she had been waiting to hear all week. "Your trial period is over," he said with mock formality. "And you'll be happy to hear you've been put on the permanent payroll. You've got the job as long as you want it. Frankly, I hope you stay for good."

"Let's talk about that in another couple of months," said Karen.

On Sunday, Lars took her to Tylosand, a seaside resort on the coast, and they lay in the warm sun and swam in the chilly Baltic Sea. On the way back, they stopped at Uppsala and had Sunday dinner with Niels and Annabelle, leaving early to get back to Stockholm before midnight. As Karen crawled into bed, slightly sunburned, she stretched contentedly and was asleep in seconds. She had never felt so sublimely happy in her life. Although Lars was quite businesslike at the office, he had never once been short with her, and he had given her ample praise for her work. They had eaten most of their meals together, and she found their relationship deepening, with the bond of working together strengthening their compatible moments after office hours. Their understanding of one another became almost instinctive, only adding to the warmth of their mutual feelings.

Karen grew to realize that while Lars certainly had his moments when he felt drawn to be close to her, to kiss her (as he had several times before saying good-night—, he was primarily a dedicated man, totally wrapped up in his work, intent on giving the best creative effort to the projects he was involved in. She remembered reading once how most creative men and women sublimate their emotions, and are, as a result, not overly aggressive in pursuing any romantic entanglement; she could only presume that Lars was too engrossed in his work to allow himself to let go, to express himself in the manner which she felt any other man might do. But she was thankful. She did not want to mar their friendship by refusing to comply with any intimacy he might suggest; there would be time enough for that, later.

She felt, with a passing twinge of awkwardness, that Lars' co-workers at the Center took it for granted that they were lovers, a feeling stemming from the sly formality with which the other men treated her. There were several other young designers on the same floor with Lars, all single, yet one of them approached her with the suggestive remarks that she remembered from working in her father's office, where every man seemed to make a pass at her. Perhaps it was the difference between European men and Americans, she thought: there was more formality in Sweden, more propriety compared with the usual looseness of office camaraderie in the States. Or maybe it was just that they concluded she belonged to Lars and were maintaining a respect for her position. The thought was quite titillating, and she would often giggle to herself over it; but she never shared her suspicions with Lars. In fact, she managed to steer their conversations away from their personal involvement, feeling that they had both reached a comfortable stage in their relationship where nothing had to be explained, nothing was taken for granted.

She would usually lunch with Lars in the cafeteria in the basement of the Center, but on the Tuesday, Lars had to fly to Goteborg for a conference. For the first time since she started work, Karen found herself lunching alone. She had just finished her dessert when she heard an exclamation of surprise, and the tall figure of Gunnar Lindstrom approached her, tray in hand. "Well, well, we meet again," he said. "Mind if I join you?"

"Not at all," she replied, moving her empty plates to one side to make room for him. "Lindstrom, wasn't it? Gunnar?"

"Right. And you? Karen? I may call you Karen, mayn't I? Or would your lord and master object?" he added with ahint of mockery in his rich, deep voice. "Where is he, by the way?"

"Of course you may call me Karen. And Lars isn't my lord and master. Just my employer. And my friend, of course."

"Employer? You mean you work at the Center?"

"Yes. I've been here over a week already. Thanks to you, really. You gave me the idea of asking Lars for a job. He's out of town today, by the way. He'll be back this evening."

"Oh." Gunnar took a bite from his sandwich

and chewed slowly, his eyes never leaving her face. "So Lars hired you after all? Wise man. I always believe we work better with a good secretary to inspire us. If I'd known you were available, I'd have asked you myself." He frowned. "But I thought you were going to school?"

"I will be," Karen replied. "But I can't get in until the fall semester. So I thought a job would be a good idea. You know, help me with the language, and getting to know the people."

"Oh. I see. You're new to Sweden, then?"

"Yes. My first trip. And I'm loving it," she said, her face radiating with pleasure. "The people are wonderful and...well, it's all like a dream come true." She looked down at her plate self-consciously. "Of course, Lars has been showing me around a lot, which has helped."

"I bet he has. He's a very talented man. He's going to make a big name for himself one of these days."

"You know his work, then?"

"Of course. My father's company has used many of Lars' designs. We tried to hire him a few years ago, but he turned us down. He said he prefers it here at the Center. More creative freedom, he said, or some such nonsense."

"I think Lars knows what he's doing," Karen replied hotly, feeling somewhat affronted by Gunnar's sneering tone of voice.

"Obviously, he does. But we would hve paid him far more than he makes here."

"Perhaps there were other considerations that are more important than money."

"Oh, ho, you do rise to his defense, don't you?" Gunnar chuckled and stared at her appraisingly. "But then, Lars is known for the loyalty he inspires in his co-workers, especially the women."

"Which is perfectly natural," Karen retorted smoothly. "He is a very attractive man."

"And you, my dear, are a most attractive young woman. If you ever get tired of working here, give me a call. I'd hire you in a second."

"Thank you for the offer, but I'm quite happy where I am." Karen sipped her coffee. "By the way, do you work here, too?"

Gunnar burst our laughing. "Dear me, no. I'm only visiting. I drop in occasionally to discuss various projects. You see, the designers here produce plans for various items that we use in our company. I can sometimes give them ideas that help overcome a particular problem."

"And they do have problems, don't they?" Karen smiled, remembering the hours she had already seen Lars poring over a drawing board, racking his brains. "But then, industrial design takes a lot of time and talent. Like this project Lars is working on now: some contract that's supposed to be especially important. And obviously, from what I've overheard, Lars is the chief designer on the project."

Gunnar swallowed the last of his sandwich, swallowed a quick gulp of coffee and patted his lips with the paper napkin. He eyed her intently. "Would this, by any chance, be the pilot nuclear plant near Leksand?" he asked casually.

"I think so, but I'm not sure."

Gunnar nodded. "If it is, Lars has my sympathies. The design is running into all sorts of difficulties, from what I've been told. Something to do with the area it's to be built in. It seems these plants require an excessively deep foundation, together with a lot of available water to cool the reactor. Oh, but you wouldn't be interested in all these technical details. Tell me about yourself. That's fare more interesting, I'm sure."

"Nothing to tell, really. My parents passed away and I've come to Sweden to live and finish my studies. Archeology."

"Yes, I remember you said that the other day when we met. That must be quite a shock to you, moving from America to Sweden."

"Not really. My uncle lives here. In Uppsala. So I feel I do have some family ties in this country. In any case, my folks came from Sweden originally, so it's really like coming home."

Gunnar nodded. "It's a good place to call home, too," he remarked, picking up a fork and toying idly with it as he spoke. "I've lived here all my life and wouldn't trade it for any other place in the world. And I've seen most of them, too." He dropped the fork and reached for his cigarettes in his shirt pocket. "Tell me, have you seen much of the country since you've been here?"

"A little," Karen replied. "Last weekend Las took me to Tylosand, which was beautiful."

Gunnar chuckled. "Did you swim in the Baltic?"

"Yes, and just about froze. But the sun was warm, though." Karen laughed at the memory. "We also visited Gripsholm Caste, which was incredible."

Gunnar nodded enthusiastically. "Oh, there are hundreds of places to see in Scandinavia. And some of the old ruins should interest you particularly, if you're interested in archeology." He glanced at his watch. "Oh, I have to run. I have a meeting at one. By the way," he paused, "would I be intruding in something if I asked you to dinner one night?"

Karen shook her head. "Not at all. I think I might enjoy that very much," she replied.

"How about tonight?"

"Well, Lars said he wouldn't be back until late..." She hesitated. "Yes, tonight would be fine. Thank you very much."

"The pleasure will be mine. Can I pick you up here at five?"

"Yes. A little earlier, if you prefer. I don't have much to do today with Lars away from his desk."

"I think we'd better make it five. There's no telling how long I'll be tied up with this meeting." Gunnar stood up and bowed his head slightly, a habit Karen remembered from their last meeting, and one that was rather charming, she thought. "I'll pick you up in front of the Center at five."

"I'll be there."

Karen returned to her office, her heart beating a little faster as she mulled over her meeting with Gunnar Lindstrom. She had remembered him as handsome, but the combination of looks and vibrant personality had not registered until now, after they had been able to get to know each other a little better. And despite the critical remarks Lars had made about Gunnar, Karen felt that they may have been grossly exaggerated, because she found Gunnar extremely charming. After all, hadn't she accepted a dinner invitation from him? And why shouldn't she? She still had strong feelings for Lars, but felt there was no harm in going out with other men, particularly one as attractive and personable as Gunnar Lindstrom.

She took out some reports she had to type, and completed them quickly, forcing the thought of the impending engagement with Gunnar from her mind as she concentrated on the content of the report, which was highly technical. But once she had finished, she tidied her desk, got herself a cold drink from the machine by the elevators, and sat relaxing and speculating over the evening ahead.

She knew, almost instinctively, that Lars would not approve of her going out with Gunnar. He had already expressed his disapproval of the man, but so what? She had an evening to herself and she hoped Lars didn't expect her to sit home alone, awaiting his return from Goteborg. Besides, she rationalized, going out with other men would broaden her knowledge of the customs and habits of the Swedes. Lars was not her infallible oracle. There were other men with other ideas which would benefit her adjustment to her new life.

Of course, she knew Gunnar probably had ideas that revolved around her availability, but if he became too aggressive, she felt she could handle that situation without any trauma. And in any case, it was only Lars' jealousy that was prompting his criticism of Gunnar, she felt sure. Until Gunnar gave her any reason to avoid him, she felt she would enjoy his company.

She was relaxing in her chair, gazing out the window when she heard the click-clack of high heels on the floor and a familiar voice call her name. She swung around, beaming with delight as a portly figure in a blinding red linen suit descended upon her.

"Annabelle!" Karen rose and embraced the other woman delightedly. "What a happy surprise! What brings you to Stockholm?"

Annabelle subsided into a chair, breathing heavily. "I decided to come in for some shopping this afternoon," she said. "And your uncle told me expressly to pop in and make sure all was well with you. It is, I gather, judging from the way you look. In fact, my dear, you look absolutely radiant." She gave Karen a questioning look and giggled salaciously. "You wouldn't by any chance be making music with Lars, would you?"

Karen flushed. "Annabelle, you know better than that. We do see each other every day, but as far as anything else...we're just very good friends. That's all, believe me."

"I don't, but we'll let it pass for the moment."

"It's true. And he's not the only man in my life," Karen said, lifting her chin defensively, "In fact, I have a dinner date this evening with someone else. Someone extremely handsome and very, very charming."

"Oh. Anyone I know?"

"Gunnar Lindstrom."

The facetious sparkle left Annabelle's eyes and she pursed her lips grimly. "Gunnar Lindstrom? Now how did you get involved with him?"

"I'm not involved. I'm just having dinner with him. Lars is out of town today and won't be back until late. Why? You know Gunnar?"

"Who doesn't?" Annabelle laughed dryly. "He's only the most talked-about bachelor in Scandinavia. Just about the richest, too. And, if you don't mind a word of warning, he has a positively obscene reputation with women."

"Gossip. Just gossip."

"Where's there's smoke, there's usually a few smouldering embers," said Annabelle. "And if he runs true to form, he'll probably want you to blow those embers into a roaring blaze before the evening's out. Mark my words, Karen, you're playing with fire by going out with Gunnar Lindstrom."

"I think I can take care of myself, Annabelle."

"Maybe so, but just watch yourself in the clinches. I've never met the man, but I've seen pictures of him, and I won't deny he's a corker. I even got a-twitter myself looking at that face of his, but then, from what I've heard, he doesn't have too much respect for women. To him, they're playthings—like any other bauble he feels he wants to buy with his money. He is disgustingly rich, you know?"

Karen nodded. "I've heard."

"Does Lars know you've met Gunnar?"

"It was Lars who introduced us," Karen replied, "but it was unavoidable. He did warn me, however. Lars doesn't like Gunnar, that I do know."

"Then, for heaven's sake, why risk offending Lars by going out with the man? A bird in the hand's worth two on the dance floor, my dear. And if I were you, I'd hang on to Lars. He's a wonderful man and he obviously likes you a great deal."

"I like Lars, too Annabelle." Karen sighed. "But I don't want to restrict myself. I mean, I'm not planning on settling down just yet."

"You want to spread your wings a little, eh?" Annabelle nodded understandingly. "Very well, my dear. Just make sure you don't get your feathers singed in the process. And if you want my advice, I wouldn't do anything to antagonize Lars. Keep him at arm's length if you must, but hang on to him. You never know when you may change your mind about settling down. I know when I was in my teens, I swore I'd stay single until I was at least twenty-five. Then my husband entered my life, and all those good intentions evaporated overnight. And as far as I'm concerned, you couldn't find a better man than Lars Tengborn."

"I know." Karen looked at Annabelle doubtfully. "But I still want to wait awhile."

"You don't sound very convincing, my dear." Annabelle got to her feet. "Well, I must be off. I have some things to get and I want to head back to Uppsala in time to fix Niels' dinner tonight. Good seeing you, Karen. Take care."

"Give my love to Uncle Niels."

"I shall. See you soon, I hope."

She threaded her way through the desks and out the door. Karen sat still, pondering over their conversation. Admittedly, she knew Annabelle was right. There could well be repercussions from Lars over her going out with Gunnar; but if he was jealous of Gunnar, he would probably be just as jealous of anyone else.

And if Lars was going to get upset over her dating other men, that was just too bad. He would have to accept the fact that she was not tied down to him. And until he asked her to marry him, she was still a free agent. She could come and go as she saw fit, and go out with whomever she chose. There would be other men in her future, she felt sure; but for the moment, it happened to be Gunnar Lindstrom, who still reminded her so very much of Kevin: the same dark good looks and muscular body, the same aura of ebullient self-confidence, the same ability to arouse that age-old yearning in her heart...So what if he had a reputation? Any man who looked like him and had the enviable freedom of choice provided by his position and money, would undoubtedly be the subject of gossip. And, Karen knew, gossip was very seldom founded on fact, but on exaggerated rumors stemming from jealousy and envy. So until the man gave her any cause for rejecting him, she would accept him on face value. And what a face...

The afternoon passed slowly, and Karen wished Lars had left more work for her to complete. She hated being idle. Finally, after what seemed an eternity, the hands of the clock pointed to four-fifty, and she decided to leave. There was no sense sitting at her desk any longer. She rose, gathered her coat and her handbag and made her way downstairs to the front entrance of the Center. She looked around, and, parked at the curb, she saw a sleek, red Alfa-Romeo standing, with Gunnar behind the wheel, waving at her.

With a happy smile, she hurried forward and slid into the low-slung bucket seat next to him.

"Been waiting long?" she asked cheerfully.

"Only about five minutes," he replied, starting the car and easing into the outside lane of traffic. "All set for a night out?"

"Not a night out," Karen replied off-handedly, trying to keep her voice light and casual. "Just dinner."

He chuckled. "The best part of dinner is what comes after," he replied, maneuvering the little sports car expertly in and out of the crush of cars heading towards the expressway.

"I'm a working girl," she answered. "I can't stay out late on a week night."

"Whatever you say," Gunnar replied. "Anyway, I thought you might enjoy dinner at Skansen Park. It's one of the islands in the harbor. Very rustic and picturesque. And the food at the restaurant is quite good."

"That sounds like fun."

"I hope it will be." He stole a quick glance at her and smiled. "But then, doing anything with you should be fun."

Karen flushed and turned away, deciding to ignore his remark, and concentrate on the passing scenery. The downtown highrise buildings were soon left behind as they approached the harbor area, chock-a-block with warehouses, smoke-grimed brick buildings and the tall skeletal latticework of the cranes, arching over the quay. As they drove by, Karen could see, at the end of the narrow streets leading to the dock, the outlines of many ships moored to the jetties.

Gunnar drove almost to the end of the harbor, then turned in towards the water, moving all the way down to an open area where a large, flat-bottomed ferry stood waiting. He parked the car, locked it and, taking Karen's arm, he escorted her across the parking lot to the ferry. They walked up the ricketty gangplank and on to the vessel, which reminded Karen somewhat of the old riverboats that were still operating on the Mississippi. A large saloon comprised the mid-section, with a small bridge above it where the captain stood, his hands on the wheel, awaiting their departure.

They had barely settled at a small table in the saloon when the floor shuddered and, with an ear-splitting shriek of the ship's siren, the ferry moved away from the dock and out into the harbor. Karen sat, her spirits soaring with excitement as she watched the parade of smaller ships and tugs. "Oh, this is great," she exclaimed. "How long does it take to get to Skansen?"

"About a half hour," Gunnar replied. "Just enough time to finish our drinks and relax a little."

He beckoned a steward and ordered two glasses of chilled Chablis, then leaned back and lit a cigarette, studying Karen intently.

"I wish you wouldn't stare at me like that," she said.

"I can't help it. You're very lovely."

"Please. No flattery. Just let's enjoy the outing."

"Very well, but you can't blame me, really."

"Nonsense! From what I've heard, you're always seen in public with only the most beautiful girls in Stockholm. So I can't be anything unusual for you," she added crisply.

"True. But every woman has her particular appeal. And you, being American, have that certain difference that intrigues me. A sort of freshness, unspoiled and unaffected."

"That has nothing to do with my nationality. That's just me." Karen sipped her wine carefully.

"By the way, what have you been hearing about me? You obviously have, from your remark a moment ago."

"Only that you're Sweden's most eligible bachelor with an eye for the ladies," Karen replied, her eyes twinkling merrily. "In fact, you seem to have quite a reputation, Mr. Lindstrom."

"It's all true," he answered with a grin, "even the lies."

They laughed and Karen relaxed. Much as she knew he was trying to pave the way for an intimate evening, she rather enjoyed his attentions, blatant as they might be. And she was enjoying the ferry ride, and had no doubt that the dinner was going to be another pleasant new experience. In fact, she slowly relaxed, letting herself blend with the mood of the moment. No tensions. No concerns over his intentions. They were just two young people out for a carefree evening. So why complicate it with apprehensions over the ultimate outcome of the evening?

"There. That's Skansen." Gunnar pointed to a flat stretch of land that spread out across the water ahead of them, its outline jagged with tall trees and a few buildings. "It's really one of the prettiest islands in the harbor. A favorite rendezvous for lovers," he added with a mischievous grin.

"I'll have to remember that," said Karen, "when I get myself a lover."

"You may already have one," he replied.

CHAPTER 11

The Alfa-Romeo pulled up at the sidewalk, and Gunnar turned off the motor. "Well, young lady," he said, "I've got you home at a respectable hour." He checked his wrist-watch. "Only eleven-thirty."

"Good," said Karen. "I turn into a pumpkin at midnight and I'd hate for you to see that."

They both laughed, and Karen opened the door and stepped out, closing it behind her and standing, looking down at him with a smile. "Gunnar, this has been a wonderful evening," she said. "Maybe we can do it again sometime."

"I'd like that very much," he replied. "Perhaps next week?"

"Yes. You know where I work. Give me a call."

"I shall. And thank you again for being so charming. I'm only sorry the evening has to end so soon." His eyes twinkled. "Perhaps next time I can buy you breakfast."

"After dancing all night, I presume?"

"Well, er..." He hestiated, then gave a self-conscious laugh "We could do that. Or find some other more interesting way to pass the time."

"That's enough out of you," Karen said pleasantly. "Any more suggestions like that will only get you in trouble."

"Trouble can be a lot of fun," he said mockingly.

"So I've been told," Karen replied, and with a wave of her hand, she ran up the steps into the apartment building, leaving him gazing after her with a look of disappointment on his face.

She giggled to herself as she made her way down the hallway, unlocked the door to her apartment and let herself in. She stood for a moment, her entire being glowing with happiness. It had been a totally enjoyable outing. Gunnar was attentive and his conversation, apart from the occasional innuendo, was polite and provocative. The food at the restaurant had been superb, and the atmosphere relaxed and informal. Chalk up another memorable evening, she thought. And, she realized, this had been her first date with someone besides Lars.

Whatever people might say about Gunnar Lindstrom, Karen could find no fault with his behavior. Admittedly he had made a few sly suggestions about his hopes for the night, and she would have been surprised if he hadn't; but his words had been veiled with discretion so that she couldn't possibly have taken offense. And after all, what was an evening without a few flirtatious remarks to add spice to the conversation?

She switched on the light and only then did she see the slip of paper on the floor, obviously pushed under the door. She reached down and read it quickly: "Karen—Please call me when you get home to let me know you're all right. Lars."

She chuckled. "Oh, my," she said aloud, picturing him sitting by his phone, chewing his nails and worried to death over her. Maybe she should just let him suffer, she thought wickedly. But then she realized he was only concerned for her safety, not knowing where she had been all evening. She looked at her wrist-watch. Eleven-thirty. Certainly Mrs. Nansen would be in bed by now, and Karen didn't want to disturb her just to make a phone call. Lars' apartment was only a short distance. She could walk there in five minutes. She decided to go in person rather than intrude on Mrs.

Nansen at this late hour.

She turned around, left the apartment and hurried along the sidewalk, going quickly down the block, feeling a surge of mischievous elation at the prospect of telling Lars about the evening. She knew he would probably disapprove, but there was nothing he could do. Gunnar had behaved himself, and she had come home alone at a respectable hour like any conscientious working girl.

She reached Lars' apartment and knocked at the door. She heard him move across the room inside, and a moment later, his voice came through the panels: "Who is it?"

"It's me."

The door opened and Lars stood there, his face a mixture of relief and anger. "Thank God," he said. "Come in. You've had me worried."

Karen walked into the apartment and dropped into a chair carelessly. "I can't imagine why," she said. "I merely went out for the evening." Lars closed the door and stood, breathing heavily and staring down at her. "Don't look at me like that, Lars."

"I didn't realize my concern would be so irritating to you," he said dryly.

He moved over and sat down opposite her on the couch, reaching for the cigarette which was in the ashtry. "I just wanted to make sure you were all right."

"And why shouldn't I be?"

"Because," he said, "you're a stranger here. You don't really know your way around yet, and even if you'd gone to a movie by yourself, I was afraid that..." His voice broke off. "Where were you, anyway?"

"At Skansen Island, having dinner with Gunnar Lindstrom."

His complexion darkened quickly and he frowned. "You had dinner with Gunnar?" he asked in a tight, strained voice.

"Yes. He met me in the cafeteria today and invited me out. I had a wonderful time. He's really very nice."

"And he brought you straight home?"

"Yes." Karen saw the suspicion and doubt forming in his eyes, and she felt a sudden surge of annoyance rise within her. "And stop questioning me as though I'd done something terrible. What did you expect me to do? Sit home? You were gone. Gunnar invited me out. What's wrong with that?"

"I thought you might wait until I returned and we could have gone out," he replied angrily.

"You weren't sure when you'd return. You told me so. You said it might be late." She paused for breath and they glared at each other like two combatants. "So stop acting like it's the end of the world, for heaven's sake."

"It could be as far as I'm concerned. I thought..." His voice broke off and he stood up and went over to the kitchen counter. Karen's eyes followed him and noted the open bottle of Scotch and a near-empty glass. He poured some liquor, added some water and returned to the couch, his eyes averted.

"Lars?"

He looked up and she saw the anger had faded and in its place, a look of hopeless yearning. "Karen, I told you once I was a jealous man. I'm not objecting to your going out, but to go out with Gunnar Lindstrom..." He shook his head hopelessly. "You're lucky you got home in one piece."

"Don't be ridiculous. He behaved like a gentleman and I'll probably go out with him again. I like him, Lars. We had a great time together."

"Oh, yes, I'm sure. I've heard when he wants to, he can charm the daylights out of anyone. Especially impressionable young newcomers to Stockholm," he added sharply.

"I am not impressionable. I know which end is up, Lars. And in any case, whatever I do on my own is none of your business."

"Oh. I see." He took a quick swallow for the Scotch. "If that's how you feel, then you'd better go on back to your apartment."

"Stop it!" Karen's voice rose angrily. "You're behaving like a spoiled brat. I do appreciate your concern, but you're getting worked up over nothing. You said yourself there would be nights when you'd either be working, or out of town. Are you expecting me to stay home all the time? That's ridiculous. And because I go out with another man doesn't mean I feel any differently about you."

He looked at her steadily. "And," he asked in a curiously quiet voice, "how do you feel about me, Karen?"

She was taken aback by his abrupt change of mood. He seemed almost contrite, abjectly apologetic for his previous outburst. "Well," she said, feeling slightly flustered, "I like you very much. You know that, Lars."

"You like me very much." His lip curled sarcastically. "If that isn't something now. Very much." He looked at her hopelessly. "I thought you really cared about me."

"I do, Lars. You're just about the nicest person I've met in my life. But you're not helping my feelings any by getting into a jealous snit just because I go out with someone else for an evening." She gave a short contemptuous laugh. "Am I supposed to check with you every time I decide to have date with someone?"

"All right, Karen. I'm sorry."

"I am, too. Not about going out," she added quickly, "but just about you. I didn't think you'd be the type to put me on a leash."

"I'm not."

"Well, you're certainly behaving like you are. I think I will go back to my place now. If we keep this up, we're only going to say things we'll regret." She rose and walked to the door. "Let's just forget it, Lars. I still feel the same about you, if that's any consolation."

Karen opened the door and let herself out, walking back to her apartment, feeling deflated and miserable. She had fully expected some reaction from Lars to her night out, but she never dreamed he would work himself into such a state. Then she remembered the bottle of Scotch on the kitchen counter.

He had probably returned from Goteborg, and after getting no response at her apartment, he went back home and started drinking. And if that were the case, he couldn't be held accountable for his outburst. She knew liquor could warp a person's judgment and bring any latent feelings of self-pity to the surface. Because that was the basic reason behind their confrontation: Lars was feeling sorry for himself, left alone for the evening while she had been out, enjoying herself with someone else. And after a few drinks, she knew, any man was liable to find his self-control submerged beneath a rising flood of senseless suspicion. And the fact that she had been out with Gunnar Lindstrom only added fuel to his fury.

Poor Lars! He must have really been going through hours of torment.

As she crawled into bed, still mulling over in her mind the regrettable climax to the evening, she suddenly realized, with a surge of elation, that for Lars to have behaved the way he did meant only one thing: he must be in love with her! If his true feelings were anything less than that, he would possibly have warned her again about Gunnar, told her of his concern for her safety and let it go. But his explosive outburst was too intense, his statements too strong for them to be prompted by anything less than an abiding love for her. How wonderful, she thought delightedly! What nicer feeling can there be than to be loved? But then, she thought with a slight pang of guilt, did she feel the same way about him? And if she did, what about all those firm protestations of remaining single for a few years? She remembered Annabelle's words, and wondered what she would do if Lars proposed. And if he had been planning to ask her to marry him, had she perhaps made him think twice about it because of her going out with Gunnar? Had she maybe ruined her chances with him after all? It was a disquieting thought and she frowned, pulled the sheet over her head and closed her eyes, her mind roiling with conflict. Tired as she felt, she tossed and turned for almost an hour before falling into a troubled sleep.

The next morning, Karen decided to forget the unpleasant scence with Lars, and to act as though nothing had happened. She had breakfast with him as usual in his apartment, then he drove them both to the Center. He had mumbled a half-hearted apology for his words, and then suggested they not refer to the incident again, and she had agreed, trying to be as casual as she could. By lunchtime, an extra amount of work involved them completely and their personal relations were thankfully forgotten beneath their duties. Karen noted that Lars seemed particularly tense, and had several meeting with his superiors after which his face appeared drawn and worried. She sensed that he was going through some sort of crisis involving his work, and that night at dinner, she questioned him about it, afraid that his feeling for her was affecting his capability at the Center.

"Silly," he said, relaxing into his usual genial smile. "I'm just worried about this contract, that's all. It's become a hassle, really. You see, there are several companies after the job and the designs I have are vital. Top secret, if you like," he added with a chuckle. "You've heard of industrial espionage, haven't you?"

Karen nodded. "Yes, I've read about it."

"Well, there are several big organizations who are after this particular job, but none of them knows what the designs call for. They have a rough idea, of course, but the details are only given out afterwards because...well, they're confidential at the moment."

"Does this involve the nuclear reactor at Leksand?" asked Karen hesitantly, remembering Gunnar's conversation.

Lars stared at her in astonishment. "It does, but how did you know?"

"Gunnar mentioned it," she replied.

"He did? That's interesting. His firm is one of the bidders for the construction, and I know he'd give his left arm to know the specs. You see, without the actual designs, companies can only submit blanket bids. If any one of them knew the details, they could tailor their cost factors to the penny, and probably win the contract as a result." He saw the expression of befuddlement on her face, and he laughed softly. "I can see this is all above your head, but don't worry. It'll be over this week. The bids have to be in by Friday. After that, we can all relax. In fact," he said, his face brghtening, "I've had an idea for next weekend. Provided you're not booked," he added slyly.

"As a matter of fact, I am," Karen replied impishly. "I have it down in my apointment book. A date with a talented designer who works at the Wenner-Gren Center. Now, let's see, what was his name?"

They both laughed happily, and Lars continued. "I have to get the designs to our subsidiary plant at Borlange, which is on the way to Leksand, where the reactor will ultimately be built. Leksand is on Siljan Lake, which is famous for their yearly summer production of the Miracle Play in their outdoor amphitheatre. It's a very impressive show, and I thought we might drive up there on Friday, drop the designs off at Borlange, and then go on to Leksand for the play. Then we can spend the weekend on Siljan Lake, which is one of the loveliest in Sweden. How's that sound to you?"

"Great!" replied Karen enthusiastically. "When do we leave?"

"Probably around eleven on Friday morning. We could leave after lunch, but that'll be cutting it a little fine." He thought a moment. "In fact, you'd better bring a suitcase to work Friday. You know, with enough for the weekend then we can take off straight from the Center. It will save coming back here to Farsta."

"Fine. It sounds like another wonderful weekend for us."

Lars reached out and closed his fingers around her hand. "That was nice of you to say that," he murmured. "For us, I mean."

"Of course I meant us," Karen replied warmly. "It wouldn't be any fun if I went alone, now, would it?"

"I now it wouldn't be for me," he said.

The week went by quickly, and only when she got home on Thursday night, did Karen realize she had not heard from Gunnar. He had said he would call, but she was just as thankful he didn't; she did not envision her coping with another outburst from Lars, especially now that their relationship had settled back into its former easy state. And much as she had enjoyed going out with Gunnar, she decided her situation with Lars was more important to her. She still envisioned herself dating other men when Lars might be out of town, but hopefully they would cause him less concern than he had shown over Gunnar.

Karen awoke early on Friday morning, filled with a joyful anticipation of the weekend at Siljan Lake. She packed a small suitcase and made her way to Lars' apartment to find him equally excited over the trip, with his bag already packed and standing by the front door.

Over breakfast, they discussed the journey, which Karen was surprised to discover was over 200 kilometers from Stockholm. "But it's a good highway," Lars reassured her. "We should make it in four hours, easily. I'll even let you drive part of the way, if you like."

"Oh, dear!" Karen pouted at him. "I must be moving up in your estimation. I thought you said once you'd never let me touch your car."

"I've changed my mind."

"I wonder why."

"I'll leave that to your imagination," he retorted teasingly.

They arrived at the Center and Karen busied herself with cleaning up the paperwork on her desk, trying to get everything done before they left. Lars disappeared to an early morning conference and promised to be through by ten-thirty. The clock on the wall pointed to a few minutes after ten when he returned, his face somber and sullen as he plumped into a chair next to Karen's desk.

"Hate to tell you this," he began. "I have to stay for an urgent meeting at one o'clock."

Karen gave a little groan. "Oh, Lars, that means we can't go...?" she began, but he cut her short.

"It means I can't go," he said abruptly, "but those plans have to be in Borlange today." He hesitated, eyeing her steadily. "If you don't mind, you could go on, deliver the plans and I'll meet you in Borlange this evening."

She stared at him uncomprehendingly. "You mean..." She hesitated, floundering hopelessly. "I don't understand, Lars. How will I get to Borlange?"

"Fly, of course. There's a flight at one-thirty. I'll follow in the car as soon as I shake loose from the meeting, pick you up at the airport in Borlange and then we can go on to Leksand just as we planned. You don't mind, do you?"

"Of course I don't mind," she said eagerly, "but what about when I get to Borlange? I still have to get to the plant there."

"Take a taxi, silly."

"Oh, of course." She smiled self-consciously.

"I'm sorry. I wasn't thinking. And you'll be up later in the car, right?"

"Yes. If for any reason I'm delayed, or if I have an accident—you never can tell—just go to the nearest hotel and check in. In fact, the Wentzhuis is only about a mile from the airport, as I remember. I've stayed there before. It's very nice."

She nodded. "Wait for you and if you don't arrive...by, what? Six o'clock? Seven?"

"I'd say seven, to be on the safe side."

"All right. If you're not at the airport by seven, I'll go to the Wentzhuis Hotel and wait there till I hear from you."

"Check." He grinned at her. "I do appreciate this, Karen."

"It's nothing. And it'll be fun, I'm sure." Her eyes sparkled excitedly. "I'll also get a chance to see more of Sweden from the air. So don't you worry."

"I won't. I know you can handle it. I've got a smart young woman working for me, remember!"

"I'm glad you think so," she retorted with a chuckle. "Just remember that when raises are handed out."

"All right." His face grew serious. "The designs are in a sealed envelope on my desk. Here." He leaned over and gave them to her. "The address is on the label, so you'll have no problems. Just make sure they get there before five.'

"I have one question," she said, frowning. "If for any reason I get delayed—you know, flight delays or whatever—and I don't get this envelope there by five, will tomorrow morning be soon enough?"

Lars pursed his lips and thought for a moment. "To be quite honest," he told her. "The deadline is Monday morning, but I would like them delivered today, just to be on the safe side. But if something happens, like you said, tomorrow would be all right."

"Okay. Just wanted to make sure."

"Fine. You can pick up some money at the cashier's office on your way out. I've made arrangements for that. And they'll also have you plane ticket for you."

"Don't worry. I'll take care of everything."

"Good, and hopefully I'll see you this evening." He stood up. "I must get back to the conference now. So have a good flight and..."

"And you drive carefully," she interrupted him with a smile.

"I will."

He walked out of the office and Karen sat for a moment stunned by the developments. She felt a tingling excitement at the unexpected turn of events, and was even more thrilled by Lars' trust in giving her the assignment. She knew the designs were crucial to the success of the project; that the contents of the envelope lying on her desk were confidential, almost top secret, and that there were probably many companies who would give anything to see them. And here she was, an insignificant assistant, charged with the responsibility of delivering them!

She rose, put the envelope in the top drawer of her desk, locked it, and made her way to the cashier's office. She picked up her plane ticket, enough money to cover her expenses, and decided to go downstairs to the cafeteria for an early lunch and then take a taxi to the airport, the Bromma Airport, she realized, which would mean she would see Stockholm from the air—another unexpected thrill!

She entered the line, got herself a bowl of soup and a ham sandwich and some coffee and made her way to a table. She had barely sat down when she heard a familiar voice, and she looked up into the smiling face of Gunnar Lindstrom. Without asking, he sat down.

"You know something," he said in a conspiratorial voice, "we'll have to stop meeting for lunch like this. People will talk."

She laughed happily. "Hello, Gunnar. How've you been?"

"Fine, just fine," he said, unloading his tray and reaching for the sugar. "And you? I've been meaning to call you, but I've been terribly busy. In fact. I'm snatching a bite now and then dashing to the airport."

"Bromma?" she asked.

"Why, yes. I'm flying up to Leksand to attend to some business."

Karen stared at him, wide-eyed. "Isn't that odd?" she said, "I'm going that way myself."

"You are?"

"Yes. I'm flying to Borlange on the one-thirty flight."

Gunnar's hand paused in midair, holding his sandwich, then he slowly lowered it and shook his head, chuckling. "I don't believe it," he murmured. "This is a coincidence." Why? You on the one-thirty flight, too?"

"Oh, no. I have my own private plane. But I am going through Borlange."

They both burst out laughing. "Oh, dear, what a small world it is," Karen said.

"Tell you what," Gunnar continued. "Why don't you come with me? It'll save your plane fare."

"It's paid for," she replied. "and I'm on company business. Thanks, anyway."

"Come on, what difference does it make? You'll be saving them some money and have some agreeable company on the way. I'm a very good pilot, by the way. I've flown all over Europe." He saw the mounting indecision on her face. "You needn't be afraid. And I promise I'll get you to Borlange at the same time, if not sooner. And I'd welcome the company, believe me."

"Well..." Karen thought a moment. It would certainly be fun, she thought. She had never flown in a private plane before and it would, she surmised, be more comfortable than being squashed into a commerical carrier. And she would get there just the same. And, she realized, Lars need not know about it until afterwards, and he certainly shouldn't have any objections. She would get there in time to deliver the envelope and be back at the airport to meet him...

"I accept," she said, her face and voice expressing her rising delight.

"I thought you would," replied Gunnar.

CHAPTER 12

They separated at the elevators, Gunnar going down to the parking lot beneath the building to get his car; Karen going back upstairs to her office for her coat and the all-important envelope to be delivered in Borlange.

Five minutes later, she scurried down the steps in front of the building and saw the gleaming red Alfa-Romeo waiting at the curb. She climbed in and settled back as Gunnar pulled out into traffic and headed for the Bromma airport, a short six miles away on the expressway. He glanced curiously at the envelope she tucked beneath the seat. "Is that the company business?" he asked casually.

She nodded. "Some papers I have to deliver to the plant in Borlange," she said briefly. "They have to get there today."

"They must be important," he observed with a sly grin.

"They are," she replied.

"In that case," Gunnar said, "why not put them in my briefcase? They'll be safer there."

"Good idea." Karen leaned over to the back seat, clicked open the small piece of luggage and slid the envelope inside.

The traffic was relatively light, and within twenty minutes they had pulled up in the parking lot of the airport, and were hurrying across the field to a row of executive planes parked behind one of the hangers. Gunnar led the way to a small single-wing aircraft and opened the door. "Okay, up you go," he said cheerfully, giving her his hand and helping her inside. He closed the door and went round to the other side and got in. "Buckle up," he said. "I'm sorry there are no stewardesses to serve you drinks, but I do have a small selection in the cooler behind the seat, if you like."

Karen shook her head. "No, thanks. I'm fine." She strapped the seat belt around her, and leaned back, her eyes sparkling with excitement as Gunnar started the engine and eased the plane forward slowly on to the runway. They sat a few minutes, awaiting clearance from the tower; then, in response to the impersonal voice that crackled over the radio, Gunnar started the plane down the seemingly endless stretch of concrete ahead of them, faster and faster...Karen clung to the edge of the seat, biting her lips nervously, her heart beating like a trip hammer. Then, with an imperceptible lifting sensation, they were airborne and zoomed up into the sky. Karen gasped, then smiled at the incredible feeling of flight, more pronounced than she had ever experienced before. "Oh, this is fantastic!" she exclaimed.

Gunnar chuckled delightedly. "This is your first time in a small plane?" he asked, raising his voice above the noise of the engine.

"Yes. I never realized what it was like. I feel like a bird."

He laughed. "I know. That's why I have my own plane. It's far more fun than riding one of those flying busses."

Karen looked down at the sprawling city of Stockholm below, and despite the thrill of the moment, she felt a twinge of disappointment. Stockholm did not look that different from Minneapolis, she thought, with its tall modern buildings, its rows of older apartments and, in the distance the prim little houses with patches of garden separating them into orderly rows. And, as they turned north and headed into the country, she saw Malaren Lake, and a series of smaller lakes, not unlike Minnesota. Then she realized with a tug at her heart, why she felt so at home here: not only the city, but the country itself, reminded her of her childhood years in another land, far across the sea...

They flew on in silence, the noise of the engine precluding any conversation. She did not mind. She was too engrossed at looking down at the exquisite panorama that slid by beneath them, the brilliant green of the fields and trees, the occasional flash of red from a barn behind a stark white farmhouse, all interlaced with the gray concrete expressways and dark-blue asphalt side roads. She saw the cars and trucks moving far below, and pictured Lars driving the Volvo up that same expressway in a few hours... She hoped there would be no need for her to confess her change of plans, for she knew, with a twinge of guilt, that he might well be angry with her—not because of the way she was traveling, but because of the man who sat behind the controls, his handsome, firm features concentrating on their flight...

And she understood completely why Lars could be so jealous. Gunnar was undeniably attractive in every way. Looks. Build. Status. Personality. He had everything, she felt, that any girl could want in a man. And while she considered Lars equally appealing, there was a basic difference between then. Gunnar was the macho, sensual type. Lars was more the aesthetic, cerebral man. Two opposites. So what if Gunnar had a bad reputation with women? She certainly had been given no reason to find him objectionable. More importantly, she *felt*

comfortable around him; not, perhaps, as clos
and affectionate as she felt with Lars, but then, sh
and Lars had been together almost every day an
most evenings. It was only natural for her to hav
developed a warmer feeling for him than for Gun
nar; she could easily be drawn closer to Gunnar i
they continued to see each other in the future
which, she knew, was quite possible. Unless, o
course, Lars brought the whole matter to a head b
asking her to marry him...

Gunnar touched her arm, and she turned t
him. He pointed down. "Borlange," he sai
loudly, and Karen frowned in disbelief. On a regu
lar jet, she had always found time passed s
slowly, almost boringly; yet here they were, almos
at their destination, and it seemed they had onl
just taken off from Bromma. Time certainly flie
when you're enjoying yourself, she though
happily.

She felt her ears popping as the plane des
cended, and as they were buffetted slightly b
crosswinds, her stomach seemed to rise to he
throat. She glanced apprehensively at Gunna
once or twice, and he grinned knowingly, an
patted her arm reassuringly. "Relax," he said
"We'll soon be on the ground."

Taking off had been a wondrous thrill, sailin
up into the sky like a bird ecstatically soaring int
the heavens; but as they dropped, closer and close
to the airport, which seemed like a miniscule do
on the ground, Karen found herself clutching th
edge of her seat, pressing her feet against the floo
and tensing up in anticipation of the fina
moment when they would plummet to earth like
falling star. Her eyes widened as the strip of con
crete rushed at them, it seemed, faster and faste

hen with a faint bump, the wheels touched down and they were moving towards the hangars, gradually slowing down and finally coming to a stop. She let out an explosive gasp of relief and smiled weakly at Gunnar, who was grinning broadly at her obvious discomfort. "That...that was something," she said lamely, her voice tremulous.

"You get used to it," he replied gruffly. He reached behind the seat for his briefcase, opened the cabin door and stepped down. Her fingers shaking, Karen undid her seat belt and, as he opened the door, she slid out, feeling his strong hand on her arm, steadying her until she was able to stand without the sensation that her knees were about to give way. "You all right?" he asked.

She nodded. "Yes, I'm fine now. The landing scared me at little, though." She took a deep breath, swallowed hard and felt her ears pop once more.

"Come on, I'll buy you a cup of coffee," Gunnar said, leading her across the landing strip to the small coffee shop on one side of the terminal. As they entered the building, Karen excused herself.

"I'll join you in a minute," she said. "I have to go to the restroom."

Five minutes later, feeling more composed, Karen walked into the small, brightly-lit coffee shop and saw Gunnar, seated by the window, smoking a cigarette and looking out at the landing strip where a small private plane was just leaving the ground. The noise of the engine died away as she sat down and took a sip from the coffee that was awaiting her.

"Better?" Gunnar said humorously, his eyes staring at her with just a trace of mockery.

She nodded. "I've got my land legs back again."

She laughed self-consciously. "It...it was quite an experience," she said.

"You didn't like it?"

"Oh, yes. The flight was wonderful. The landing scared me a little, though. I felt as though we were coming down too fast, like we were going to crash. I know that's stupid, but..."

"I know. In a jet, you're not aware of the descent as you are in the cockpit of a small plane. There's no need to be afraid, ever. If the engines go out in a jet, you're done for. In a small plane, you can glide down safely and land."

He leaned back, stubbed his cigarette carelessly in the ashtray and smiled at her. "Well, what now?"

"I'll be on my way," she replied. "Oh, the envelope, before you take off with it."

"Of course." He clicked open the attache case, slid his hand inside and extracted the brown manila package and handed it to her. "You will take a plane back to Stockholm after you deliver this?"

She hesitated. "Er..no," she answered carefully. "I'll be staying over, I think."

"Oh. Where?"

She thought quickly, then remembered the name of the hotel Lars had told her. "At the Wentzhuis."

Gunnar nodded. "I know it. A rather nice place, actually, though quite small. Tell you what, why don't you deliver your package, and then we can go to the hotel and have a drink and some dinner. Then I'll fly on afterwards."

"Oh, no, that won't be necessary," Karen said quickly. "I'll just get a taxi in a minute and be on my way. You have your business in Leksand. You'd better be flying on before dusk."

Gunnar shook his head. "I've got nothing that can't wait," he said smoothly. "Besides, you're not going to deny me the pleasure of buying your dinner, surely?"

"It's not that," Karen said wretchedly, feeling the situation slowly slipping out of her control; her inherent honesty rose to the surface and she decided to brazen it out. "To be quite honest, Gunnar, I'm being picked up later. So there's no sense your staying, really."

"Oh-ho." He stared at her steadily with a knowing gleam in his eyes. "It sounds like my rival has already staked his claim, eh?"

She flushed. "If you must know, Lars is driving up later and we're going to the Miracle Play at Leksand."

"And probably spending the rest of the weekend on the lake?" She remained silent, looking down at her coffee cup, and he nodded. "So be it. I'm not going to rock the boat, Karen. But I have a confession to make." She lifted her eyes and looked at him curiously. "You see," he continued, "after the other night, I just couldn't get you out of my mind. That's why I haven't called you, really. I knew if I started seeing you too often, I'd fall even more in love with you than I am already. No, don't say anything." He raised his hand to silence her instinctive protest. "It sounds ridiculous, perhaps, but happens to be true. I've known a lot of women in my time, Karen, but nobody's affected me quite the way you have. If I hadn't run into you today in the cafeteria, you'd have probably never head from me again. You see, I'm not the marrying kind. I plan to settle down one day, but not just yet. And I knew that would be the only arrangement you would go for, so..." He shrugged. "I knew it was useless to continue seeing you. I'd only be torturing myself." He smiled wryly." I've never been the masochistic type." He pushed his chair back. "But as we've come this far, do have dinner with me tonight. Just one more time. A farewell occasion," he added with a touch of sadness in his voice.

"Gunnar..." Karen's mind whirled, hardly able to believe what she had heard. "I..."

"Please. Just this once?"

His eyes were pleading, his voice touchingly sincere, and Karen felt her resistance melting. Unexpected as they were, his words had broke through the brittle wall of resistance she had built up against the thought of any deep involvement with him. She thought she might possibly see him again, but she hadn't counted on such a confession coming from someone like Gunnar. He sounded and looked like an infatuated teenager rather than the hedonistic man-about-town, and, somewhat reluctantly, she felt the least she could do would be to have dinner with him that night. An early dinner, she thought quickly, so she could get back to the airport in time to meet Lars.

"Very well," she agreed finally. "But only if we get back here by seven. And please, Gunnar, I'd rather not hear anything else about your feelings for me. I'm touched. I really am. But..."

"Say no more. I understand."

"Thank you," she said gratefully, standing up and reaching for the envelope. "Now I must get this to the plant."

They walked through the small terminal and Gunnar signalled a taxi to the sidewalk. They climbed in and Karen gave the address to the driver, who nodded, and pulled out towards the roadway. She stared out the window, admiring the small country homes and the wide expanse of meadows and fields, some with cattle grazing leisurely in the waning afternoon sunshine. Gunnar, wisely, refrained from conversation, and she was thankful. His confession had left her visibly shaken, and she felt the dinner might well be an endurance course in verbal fencing; but it was the least she could give him, she felt, in return for his kindness in flying her to Borlange.

Within ten minutes the taxi pulled up in front of a modest looking industrial plant. "I'll just be a minute," she said, jumping out and running up the short flight of steps to the plate glass front door. She went over to a reception desk, where a middle-aged woman in glasses looked up at her, smiling.

"I think you're expecting this," Karen said. "It's from Lars Tengborn at the Wenner-Gren Center in Stockholm."

The woman took the envelope, looked at the label and nodded. "Thank you very much," she said. "I'll see it gets into the right hands at once. They've been waiting for this," she added.

Karen turned and went back outside, a vague sense of relief at having completed the delivery before five o'clock, as Lars had wanted. She got back in the taxi feeling quite cheerful, and in minutes they were back on the highway, heading for the Wentzhuis Hotel.

Gunnar was quiet, saying little until they had settled in the hotel diningroom with a bottle of wine between them. "So you and Lars are going to the Miracle Play?" he said.

Karen nodded. "Yes. He says it's quite spectacular. I'm looking forward to it."

Gunnar nodded. "I saw it a few seasons ago. It is impressive." He smiled sadly. "I only wish I were taking you. There are so many things I'd like to share with you in Sweden, Karen."

"I'm sure there are, Gunnar, but for the moment, let's not complicate things."

He paused a moment, pursing his lips. "You sound as though you're quite involved with Lars."

"You might say that. He's been very good to me. And I do like him very much."

"Are you in love with him?"

She met his direct stare with complete candor and without any hesitation, she replied: "Yes, I think I am."

"Are you going to marry him?"

She nodded. "If and when he asks me."

He took a sip from his wineglass and licked his lips as he looked sadly at her. "Congratulations," he murmured softly. "I don't know which one of you is the luckier."

The waiter approached the table and they concentrated on ordering the meal. Gunnar continued making small talk, but Karen was unable to match his outward calm. She felt awkward and she knew her inner tensions showed in her expresion and her voice. But she couldn't help it. She just wanted the meal to be over so she could return to the airport and await Lars' arrival. Had she known Gunnar was so deeply drawn to her, she would never have accepted his offer to fly to Borlange. But she drew some consolation from the fact that she would not be seeing Gunnar again. At least the matter was resolved, both in his mind and her own. And she was rather surprised at her own admission to him of her feelings for Lars. Her reply to his question had been so spontaneous, so unhesitating, that she knew there could not be any further evasion on her part: she was in love with Lars. She wanted to marry him. And the sooner, the better... So despite the uncomfortable outcome of their trip, she was, in a way, grateful to Gunnar for helping her realize how she felt and what her true feelings were for Lars. He had unwittingly become a catalyst for the conflicting emotions within her. And she was happy at last to have made the decision in her own mind. Now all it needed was for Lars to get around to asking her...

"A liqueur?" Gunnar asked. "Maybe Drambuie? That's always good after dinner."

"I think not," she replied. "I'll just stick to coffee."

He ordered one Drambuie, lit a cigarette and leaned back in his chair, contemplating her with a soft smile. "What if Lars doesn't arrive?" he said suddenly.

"He will." She met his gaze with as much confidence as she could muster.

"He could be delayed. He might have a wreck. Then what would you do?"

"Stay here at the hotel until I hear from him," she replied promptly. "Then fly back to Stockholm."

"All very cut and dried, isn't it?" He stared at her and his voice suddenly became mocking. "Let's suppose, just for argument's sake, that Lars doesn't make it. You're certainly not going to feel very happy by yourself, surely? Having to spend a night alone in a strange hotel isn't the happiest experience."

"Maybe so, but I happen to enjoy reading in bed. I'm just as happy curled up with a good book."

"A book is poor company compared with a man."

"I wouldn't know about that."

He raised his eyebrows and chuckled. "Oh, come on, Karen. Stop pulling this innocent virgin act. If you've been going with Lars, you can't expect me to believe he kisses you goodnight on the doorstep and goes home like a good little boy?"

"As a matter of fact, he does," she replied hotly, feeling her anger slowly rising at his insinuations.

"I don't believe you, my dear. And I'm willing to bet if you were honest with yourself, you'd admit you want to share that lovely little body with me. I've felt it all afternoon. I'm not asking for a lifelong attachment, but I would like something more than a farewell dinner to remember you by."

Karen realized her heart had begun beating so fast, her hands were trembling. She remained silent, knowing that if she spoke, her voice would certainly betray her dwindling self-control and she had no desire to cause a scene in the dininggroom. She turned her head away and stared out the window. Her ears caught the rasp of his chair on the polished floor as he moved it suddenly closer to her, and a second later, she felt the touch of his hand on her thigh under the table. At the same instant, he leaned forward, his mouth almost touching her ear, and whispered to her. In a split second, her mind flashed back over the years, and it wasn't Gunnar next to her, but Kevin, and the memory of his heavy-handed approach, and the identical obscene remark, almost brought a cry to her lips. She pushed her chair back quickly and stood up, her knees catching the edge of the table and upsetting the glasses with a crash.

"How dare you!" She glared at his upturned face, sneering and sarcastic. "You're despicable!"

Gunnar reached out and grabbed her wrist, pulling her down impatiently. "Sit down," he rasped, "and stop making a scene."

Before Karen could reply, she heard the sound of approaching footsteps; saw Gunnar turn, a look of surprise and disbelief on his face; saw a figure push past her; saw a fist come down; and then Gunnar was sprawled on the floor, blood beginning to ooze from his lip. She looked up and felt a wave of relief chase the chilling fear in her heart.

"Oh, Lars...Lars," she whispered.

His face was a mixture of concern and anger as he reached over the table and picked up Gunnar's briefcase, opened it quickly and took out a brown manila envelope. Karen gasped as she recognized it. "But..." she started to say.

"Come on," Lars snapped, taking her hand and almost dragging her away from the table and out into the lobby of the hotel.

"Wait, Lars, please."

He paused, and stood a moment, breathing heavily. Karen looked back through the door into the diningroom and saw Gunnar getting to his feet and reaching for a napkin to wipe his mouth; then she stared at Lars uncomprehendingly.

"What's happening?" she asked faintly. "The envelope...?"

"It's all right," he said briefly. "I'll explain it all in the car."

They hurried out of the hotel and Karen saw the Volvo a short distance away in the parking lot. As they approached, she noticed the outline of two figures in the back seat. She opened the door and got in, then stared disbelievingly at the two smiling faces in the back.

"Uncle Niels... Annabelle..." Her pentup emotions gave way and she found herself weeping uncontrollably. Lars slipped behind the wheel and pulled her against his shoulder.

"I feel like such an idiot," she managed to blurt out between sobs. "What...what's going on, Lars?"

"You want to know now, or can it wait?" he said with a glance at the two curious faces behind them.

"Now, for heaven's sake." She sniffed and wiped her eyes on the back of her hand.

"Yes, we want to know, too," said Annabelle loudly. "We saw your performance through the window. Talk about cave-man tactics..."

"Are you all right, Karen?" asked Niels, leaning forward anxiously. She nodded. "I'm fine," she mumbled, "but I'd like to know what this is all about. And how come you two are here?"

"All in good time, my dear," said Niels, his eyes twinkling merrily. "I think Lars had better explain."

"Very well." Lars patted the envelope on the seat. "First of all, this. I guess you're wondering what it was doing in Gunnar's briefcase?"

Karen nodded. "How did it get there? I delivered it at the plant."

"You delivered an envelope all right, but it contained some meaningless designs that were stolen from the Center," Lars began. "You remember the night I took you up to show you the office?" She nodded. "We ran into Gunnar and I started getting suspicious then, because he really had no business in the building, and certainly not in the office where we saw him. I shared my concerns with some of the other men I work with, but they felt Gunnar would never stoop to anything like that. After all, his family is highly respected, and his firm one of the top companies in Sweden. So I let it go. But then, this afternoon, when I hit the edge of town, I called the plant to make sure you'd delivered the envelope. I felt it would save me a trip there, and I could go straight to the airport and pick you up. My associate there told me the envelope had arrived, but couldn't understand why I had sent the material that was in it. He felt here had been a mixup at the Center, but I knew differently, because I'd put the designs in the envelope myself. I knew something was seriously wrong. I went to the airport, looking for you, and, of course, you were not there. But I happened to notice Gunnar's plane parked outside the terminal, and I put two and two together. I checked with the airline and discovered you hadn't been on the one-thirty flight. I knew then you had flown up with Gunnar. How, of course, I had no idea, but that was the only solution I could think of, especially after I'd made a few phone calls and learned that Gunnar had been nosing around the Center this morning. He had asked one of the girls if he could use a typewriter, it seems, so I suspect he typed another label on another envelope, and decided to try and make a switch, which he obviously did. Did you ever leave the envelope alone where he could get to it?"

"I put it in his briefcase when we flew up," Karen said.

"Of course. And when he gave it back, he handed you the other envelope. They were identical, so naturally you didn't suspect anything."

Karen gasped. "He was using me," she gasped. "That's all it was. Just a scheme to get the designs. And to think of all he said to me..." Her voice trailed off, remembering Gunnar's heart-rending confession of his feelings for her. He hadn't meant a word of it, she realized. It was all part of his game...

"He knew I was tied up in a conference, so he figured you would be taking the designs to Borlange," Lars continued. "The only thing he could do was get them through you. How did he manage to get you to fly with him? You were booked on the plane."

"We met in the cafeteria," Karen began, but Lars broke in with a laugh. "You didn't meet," he interrupted. "He went looking for you. I know, because he asked about you upstairs. So he obviously went to the cafeteria, made his pitch and you fell for it."

"Oh!" Karen bit her lip and blushed. "How could I have been so stupid, so trusting?"

"Because you liked him, and thought he was on the level. You wouldn't listen to me, would you?" Lars said humorously. "You had to find out the hard way."

"I could have told her that." Annabelle broke in boisterously. "I've never trusted a dark man. Besides," she added with a giggle, "blondes are more fun."

"So what's going to happen to Gunnar?" Karen asked.

"There'll probably be some action taken against him," Lars replied. "Industrial espionage is a serious matter. I hope they throw the book at him."

Karen smiled shyly. "I'm certainly grateful you arrived when you did," she murmured. "He was making the most indecent suggestions to me and pawing me under the table. And to think I was beginning to really like him a lot. Oh!" She turned to the back seat. "And how come you two are here? Lars didn't tell me he planned to bring you along."

"He picked us up on the way," Niels said with a chuckle. "He felt it was the only thing to do after I told him our news."

"What news, Uncle Niels?"

"Well, next to yours, this may seem a little tame. You see, I called Lars this afternoon to invite you both for the weekend. We want you for a special reason, you see." He paused and looked at Annabelle sheepishly. "The fact is: the old girl's finally got me to say yes."

"You mean you're getting married this weekend?"

Annabelle nodded, her face glowing. "At last, my dear, at long last, yes! We're going to tie the knot on Sunday in the campus chapel. A college wedding, would you believe?"

"Oh, how wonderful!" Karen leaned over and hugged them both. "Can I be a bridesmaid?"

"Afraid not," said Lars.

"And why not?"

"Because," he replied, "you can't be a bridesmaid and a bride at the same time."

"That's telling her," said Annabelle, and Niels gave a happy laugh. "You know how we Christensens like to do things together, don't you, Karen? I thought a double wedding would be rather appropriate."

Karen gasped and looked at Lars. "Are you asking...?" she began, but he cut her short.

"Of course I am, you ninny," he said tenderly, pulling her into his arms. "You will marry me, won't you, Karen?"

"I'll have to think about it," she replied mischievously.

"Very well," he retorted. "You have five seconds to give me your answer."

She hugged him hungrily. "Oh, yes, yes," she whispered. She felt his lips cover her own, warm and demanding, and she felt her heart would explode with happiness.

"My, my," said Annabelle enviously. "You've never kissed me like that, Niels."

"There's always a first time," he replied, embracing her tightly. The car was quiet for a few breathless moments; then they all broke apart. Annabelle giggled loudly.

"Oh, dear," she murmured. "Is there a church nearby, Lars? I don't know whether I can hold out till Sunday."